The Assembly Room

Bryony Allen

First Published in 2012 by:
Pneuma Springs Publishing

The Assembly Room
Copyright © 2012   Bryony Allen
Cover artwork by Richie Cumberlidge

Pneuma Springs

British Library Cataloguing in Publication Data

Allen, Bryony.
  The Assembly Room.
  1. Suffolk (England)--Fiction. 2. Young adult fiction.
  I. Title
  823.9'2-dc23

  ISBN-13: 9781782281801

Pneuma Springs Publishing
A Subsidiary of Pneuma Springs Ltd.
7 Groveherst Road, Dartford Kent, DA1 5JD.
E: admin@pneumasprings.co.uk
W: www.pneumasprings.co.uk

For Terence John Cundall
(13.06.1934 – 14.03.2011)

'...as if some busie men had made use of
some ill Arts to extort such confession...'
(Notestein, 1911)

ACKNOWLEDGEMENT

I'd like to start by giving thanks for the undying support of my family, friends and the wonderful book reviewers and readers out there. You are the inspiration that keeps me writing and all help provide the perseverance and belief needed in the competitive world of writing fiction today. I also wish to make reference to the following books which greatly assisted me in the research carried out for the writing of this novel. The presence of these works has helped to provide the historical background of the 17th century period and its methods as depicted in this book. However be aware that imagination has twisted its way through the factual accuracy.

"Witchfinders, A Seventeenth-Century English tragedy" by Malcolm Gaskill (John Murray Publishing 2006)

"Witches in and around Suffolk" by Pip and Joy Wright (Pawprint Publishing 2009)

"The Witchfinder and the Devil's Darlings" by Simon Peters (Lucas Books 2003)

1

Looking back, Merryn wished she had trusted her instincts when she first saw The Assembly Room. She should have yelled at her father to turn round and take them back to their miserable rented house, in the most miserable estate in town, back to her miserable school. She should have told him that she could cope with her damp, tiny bedroom and the booming of music rattling pictures off her wall. She should have said that she could put up with the rubbish teachers who had given up on the idea of discipline, the gangs of children that had more power than the teachers and the universal mockery of her ambition to be a teacher.

Instead, they were stuck behind a tractor on a Suffolk country road for the third time in half an hour. She gazed out of the window looking at the area that would be her home; there was not much to see, however, if you didn't like fields, hedgerows and more green stuff, punctuated with a quaint house here and there. The place they were currently crawling past would never have made it onto the archetypal chocolate box. It would have been better placed on a trailer for 'Ghost Hunters' or 'Most Haunted'.

"I pity anyone who lives near that place!" Merryn muttered.

"What's wrong with it?" her father, Matt, asked with exaggerated indignation.

"What's right with it, more like? It's a dump!" Merryn retorted. She looked in distaste at the dirty, ramshackle building with its leaning porch and corrugated iron roof. It was a rectangular, one and a half storey structure with double Gothic-shaped entrance doors on a small side facing the road. By the side of each door was a long, arched window covered from the inside with an assortment of wood cut-offs. Above the doors was a wider window, again shabby yet heralding an ornate arch. Its name stood out proudly in brick pattern: The Assembly Room.

"I bet it's haunted," Matt continued to tease earning a glare from his wife.

Merryn took the high ground well trodden by fourteen-year-olds and chose to ignore that comment, preferring instead to tut loudly and roll her eyes. "Mum," she said. "Can you turn the heating up? I'm cold."

As Rosie, her mother, reached down for the knob, her father interjected. "How can you be cold? It's the middle of April, the sun's out and it's boiling in this car. Mind you, if you will go out without a jumper…"

Putting as much venom into the word "Dad" as she could, Merryn turned to look out of the rear window. She may not have physically increased the distance between herself and her ridiculously annoying father, but at least she had made a statement. It was fortunate that she could not see the grin on his face.

The tractor slowed to a near halt as it began to negotiate an awkward right turn and Matt was forced to stop. Merryn decided to turn round to take a final look at the run-down building. She found the ugliness of the place strangely interesting as though there was some story to be told behind those crumbling walls. As she cast her eyes over the dereliction, Merryn caught a sudden glimpse of movement at one of the boarded windows. She blinked hard and narrowed her eyes to get a closer look, but it was no use. The tractor was gone and her dad was speeding away; The Assembly Room was disappearing out of sight.

"Merryn, we've got to go to the shop first to pick up some bits. Do you need anything?" Rosie asked.

"Chocolate," said Merryn automatically. She was still thinking about that revolting old building, and whether she had actually seen something. Probably just some wildlife, she surmised with no enthusiasm at all. Now they were living in the country she would have to get used to being surrounded by all things bright and beautiful…and deadly boring.

Two minutes of following the main road through Hitcham brought them to the little village shop. Merryn wandered up and down the two long aisles that stocked everything from electrical fuses to cheap toys to baked beans. Her parents stocked up and chatted to the lady behind the counter but she paid no attention to the conversation, preferring to look at the surprisingly ample selection of magazines.

"Where are you moving to then?" asked the nosy assistant.

"Bramble Cottage opposite the Brettenham turning," announced Matt proudly. "It was my uncle's place but I guess I was the favourite nephew. Actually, that's not true. I was the only relative! Do you know where I mean?"

"Oh yes," replied the assistant. "Everyone knows Mowles' Corner."

Matt waited for her to carry on but her light-hearted gossip stopped. Instead, the woman just looked at him with a mixture of distrust and anger in her eyes. Merryn had heard people talk about cutting the atmosphere with a knife, but, until now, she did not know what they meant. It was as though someone had hit a pause button and no one was sure how, or indeed whether, to restart. Matt broke the awkward tension. He fumbled around in his pocket for his wallet, then struggled to pull out his bankcard. Clutching the bags, he muttered a dispirited goodbye to the glaring woman.

"She was a bit weird wasn't she? Don't know what I did wrong," he said to Rosie, ignoring the eyes burning holes in his back.

"Maybe they don't like new people here. Or maybe we have to pass some sort of initiation test. Not a good idea to upset the locals on our first day here, though. They might come for you in the middle of the night and sacrifice you to the gods of the harvest or something," Merryn teased, and the sombre mood was broken as her dad mock-punched her arm.

They got into their car and went back the way they had come. Very soon, they were pulling into a gravelled driveway that led to a communal parking area. Suddenly, a flash of sunlight dazzled Merryn and she had to shield her eyes. It was so intense that she could only squint at what was directly in front of her. She could see three houses: two were big and modern, painted in traditional, pastel colours and one was a beautiful Victorian farmhouse. Her heart started racing as she waited to be told which one these mini-mansions was to be her new home. But her parents were facing another direction. They were pointing towards a pair of ancient semi-detached cottages with timber frames, and dormer windows poking through threadbare thatch.

"That's ours!" Matt pointed to the first of the thatched cottages; the one with the leaded, arched windows and the Suffolk pink rendering. Merryn was speechless. It was disgusting. The windows were thick with dirt, and weeds had turned the front garden into a jungle. It was like a 'before' in a television property programme; the sort of place the presenters would not go into for fear of messing up their hair or make-up. But she managed to force a smile and grunted some sort of encouraging sound. She could not bear to dent her father's boyful enthusiasm.

For months, he had talked of nothing but their fantastic new life in the country and his amazing, lucky inheritance. This was going to be their forever home, the solution to all their problems. He promised Merryn that he would be a 'proper dad' and give her a better life, and it seemed as though he loved doing it. Matt would drop cryptic hints about his plans, set teasing quizzes and wind up his daughter to frustrating levels. He had even refused to let Merryn and Rosie visit the 'dream house' he bragged about because he did not want to spoil the surprise when they finally moved in.

His enthusiasm even managed to sweep away the few secret misgivings Merryn had about leaving the civilisation of a town. Despite her unhappiness, she protested initially and said that she would rather run away from home than move into the middle of nowhere. Then her father's infectious seeds of optimism started to spread and she began to get slightly excited at the thought of living somewhere totally different, somewhere that promised peace and quiet, somewhere she could start again with a new set of friends who might be more than just people she saw at school. Merryn would never admit that to her dad, though. With an exaggerated sulk, she accepted his promises of unlimited car rides to towns whenever she needed retail therapy and his offer of a greatly raised allowance.

"Actually," he continued, "there's more. Jump out of the car and I'll show you."

Merryn was still cupping her hands around the sides of her eyes as she grudgingly followed Matt to the front of the cottage. He was obviously not affected by the near-blinding glare as he was standing with his chest out, his shoulders back and turning his head to survey his new empire. He put his arm around Merryn and said, "We own the adjoining cottage too!"

How could he be so proud? Merryn thought as she gazed in horror at the wreck of a house. It should have been a mirror image of the house next door, but it was even worse. The rendering was broken and hanging in tatters around the wooden framework. There was no glass in any of the windows and the front door hung desolately off its hinges. The only thing that was holding that place together was faith. Those same property people would have advised demolition, and it probably wouldn't take anything more powerful than a child's plastic hammer to destroy the place. She thought of her old cornflake packet house, with its paper-thin walls, its anti-social neighbours and views overlooking a paint factory, and yearned to return to her former uncomfortable life.

"That's my pension project," her father said as Merryn began to feel slightly nauseous. "And, as for that place, that's ours too. Mind you, I've no idea yet what I'm going to do with it!"

The piercing glare of the sun vanished suddenly and Merryn could see again, though that was not a good thing. How had she not noticed that thing when they pulled into the driveway? Surely even her temporary blindness could not have hidden that hideous monstrosity. It was the awful building they had passed earlier; the building worthy of a leading role in a horror movie. Instinctively, she took a step backwards and drew her arms around her body to contain the shudder. She wanted to drag her eyes away, but she felt compelled to keep staring, to take in the aura of dereliction and neglect.

"We can't live here, Dad!" she cried.

"Oh, Merryn," soothed Matt. "I know you'll miss your friends and the old place, but this opportunity is too fantastic to pass up. We'll soon get it straight and you'll soon settle here." In true dad-style, he said what he thought were the correct words for what he thought was the problem, and shushed away her protestations. If only he had really listened.

"Go and get Snowdrop from the car. She'll be wondering what's going on, but don't let her out of the basket yet." He continued shouting instructions but they were ignored as Merryn ran back to the car, climbed in and slammed the door shut. Then she dragged her white cat out of the basket and cuddled her so tightly that she got scratched.

9

2

Merryn chose the smallest bedroom of the three, the only one at the back of the house. She mumbled something about the amazing views over the garden and the fields beyond, and she claimed to have fallen in love with the small cast-iron fireplace. Matt and Rosie chose not to question her choice, knowing better than to argue with their hormonal daughter, but they could not understand it. Her one stipulation on moving was that she got a big bedroom – this one was about half the size of what she was used to. Merryn could not tell them that she did not want to be facing The Assembly Room.

The rest of the upstairs contained two large double bedrooms and a bathroom that Rosie said must have been a later addition. Merryn did query the 'later' as it was most definitely Victorian in its fittings, down to the ornate clawed bath. The toilet even had its cistern attached high on the wall with a long chain to pull. Still, it seemed clean enough in its ancient beauty.

Merryn gasped with delight when she walked into the enormous kitchen. Again, it was very dated but beautiful. There was a butler sink underneath one of the windows, and recessed into an inglenook fireplace was a large black stove. Next to the stable door leading to the garden was a row of pine dressers, the wood chipped and smoothed with age but all the more homely for its domestic scars. It was Merryn's dream kitchen, and, as an added bonus, it was also at the back of the house.

The front door was in the centre of the house and either side of that were two equally sized, dark and dingy rooms. Matt allocated one for a study and the other for a lounge, but Merryn doubted she would use that much. She pictured those overpaid TV presenters wandering around this house, waffling about original features then simpering about the kitchen being the heart of this house.

Within an hour of their arrival, Merryn lost the luxury of wallowing in delight and fear over her new surroundings as the removal van turned up and chaos ensued. Hundreds of boxes, a mountain of confusion and several expletives later, the empty shell of their new home began to breathe life.

In her bedroom, Merryn managed to squeeze a chest of drawers next to her single bed, and tucked her desk under her window having sacrificed her wardrobe to the spare room. She brought Snowdrop in with her and opened the basket, but the cat refused to get out. Merryn knew that her pet would be reluctant to explore, but she had not been prepared for the swearing and the hissing. She had certainly not anticipated the sudden lunge of razor-sharp claws and the blood drawing scratches as Merryn reached an arm inside to soothe the fractious cat.

Going downstairs to clean the cut, she shut the door on the grumpy feline. Her mum and dad were discussing their adjoining property.

"Do you want to come over with me now and have a look?" asked a very enthusiastic Matt.

"Not at the moment," came a much less eager reply from his wife. "I've got to attempt to make some sort of meal from these packets. Whose great idea was it to live in a place with no takeaway? Besides, it's dark and there's no electricity in there."

"I've got a torch in the car," he pleaded.

But Rosie was adamant so her sulking husband turned to his daughter. "Please, please, please. I need someone to hold my hand in case there's something in there like...I don't know... a spider." He pulled what he thought was a pitiful face and knocked his knees together in mock fear, provoking no more sympathy than an exchanged look of exasperation between mother and child.

Merryn groaned, "Okay. I'll come next door with you but I won't go into that other place."

"The Assembly Room? Why not?"

"Because it's...it's disgusting and it's falling to pieces. And I bet it's haunted or something – that's why not!"

Matt laughed. "Don't be so ridiculous - I was only joking. There are no such things as ghosts, especially not in there. No self-respecting ghost would want to go in that dump. Seriously, though, it may be better if you don't go in there until I've worked out how safe it is. Right then, let's go next door and watch out for the ghosties."

Ordinarily, Merryn would have rolled her eyes at her dad's stupid ghost noises and wonder out loud if all fathers were as embarrassing. But she was too busy telling herself that The Assembly Room was only spooky because it looked so bad; that there was nothing to be afraid of. Science over superstition, she whispered over and over again. Wasn't she the one who would shout at the film, 'Paranormal Activity', saying it was all a fake?

In fact, science won the battle as they pushed open a front door that creaked and swayed on one hinge. At every step, Merryn expected some part of the house's structure to come crashing down on her head but the house would not even grant her that amount of excitement. Matt's halogen torch illuminated a downstairs that was identical to its neighbour in layout. The only other similarities however were the windows and the deep fireplaces. Elsewhere, all the oak beams and original features that were exposed in their house were hidden behind shoddy boards.

While her dad raved about what a fabulous place it was, its potential, its beauty, Merryn just saw neglect. It was an unloved wooden shell that had not been touched in centuries. It smelt of damp and decay, and had absolutely no feeling or atmosphere about it. Nothing had lived in it for centuries – not even a foolhardy field mouse. The house was dead.

"Well?" Rosie asked thirty minutes later as they sat around the kitchen table with their tea of cheese sandwiches, crisps, chocolate biscuits and coke.

"It's going to take a lot of work," sighed Matt. "I haven't got time at the moment, which is such a shame as it could be a really lovely house. But it's structurally sound enough and it's not going to go anywhere, so it will just have to stay like that for a few more years."

Matt and Rosie continued to discuss possibilities for both houses, while Merryn drifted into thoughts of her own. She had avoided looking at The Assembly Room as she walked the twenty steps between the two front doors, but she still felt its presence. She felt stupid admitting this even to herself. However, she could not shake a weird sense of foreboding. It was as though something was waiting there, watching and waiting. Merryn resolved to avoid that place at all costs. A difficult task considering how close the building was to her own front door.

3

Early the following Monday morning, Merryn walked from her front door, across the open grassed area to wait for the school bus.

"You need to be over here," called a voice from outside The Assembly Room.

Merryn looked over at a boy standing by himself. He was about the same age as her and wearing the same school sweatshirt. Her heart fluttered a bit as she assessed his brown hair that was long enough to flop over his face without looking scruffy, his mildly muscular tall frame that showed promise of a six pack and a face that reminded her of Robert Pattinson. Steeling herself against the fear of approaching The Assembly Room and the fear of how to act casually in the presence of someone so fit, she walked over to him.

"Hi, I'm Jamie," he said.

"Hi," Merryn replied nervously. "I'm Merryn." He was even more gorgeous close up. Merryn could feel herself turning red and her tongue threatened to tie itself in knots. "Is this where the school bus stops?"

But Jamie just smiled and pretended she hadn't just asked a ridiculously obvious question. "Yeah. It's always late though."

Silence fell on them, until Merryn awkwardly asked, "So what year are you in?"

"Year 10, like you. They asked me to look out for you. They've put us in the same form group. Maybe they think we country folk need to stay together in case we get lost," Jamie drawled in a yokel voice that made Merryn erupt into fits of giggles. The bus arrived to take them to nearby Hadleigh and Jamie educated a more relaxed Merryn in the essentials of school life and gossip.

"Must be tough on you being the new kid half way through a school year," he commented as he showed her the way to their form room.

"Yes and no," Merryn mused. "I will miss my mates but the school was so rubbish. The teachers were always off sick and there were always loads of fights. I'm a bit of a geek too, which didn't help."

"I wouldn't say that too loud around here," advised Jamie. "People like us have to hide our true identity otherwise we will be bully fodder for that lot." He pointed over at the stereotypical gang of social leaders taking pride of place near the lockers. They didn't worry Merryn. She had mastered the art of combining conformism and individuality, as had Jamie: an unusual but extremely beneficial accomplishment.

Merryn's first day went surprisingly okay. Jamie was with her in most of her lessons, except Maths, and he introduced her to his group of friends - a random but happy mixture of boys and girls. By the end of the day, she had swapped mobile phone numbers and e-mail addresses with all of them. Her lessons went well too, with her teachers being the usual assortment of the good, the bad, the ugly, those who were cool and those who were desperate to be cool as well as those who just did not care.

Therefore, it was with a happy heart that she returned home. Even the chill she felt from the direction of The Assembly Room could not dent her contentment. However, as she walked into the kitchen, she knew that her mum did not share her mood.

"What's up?" she asked after helping herself to a chocolate biscuit.

"It's your dad's job. The bank he works at is giving the contract to another IT company, and they won't be taking all their employees with them."

"But surely they won't get rid of Dad," reasoned Merryn. "He's been there for years."

"That's part of the problem though. He's expensive as he's been there for so long. They can get cheaper people straight from university, who don't have family commitments and are more prepared to work ridiculous hours. Your dad has always put us first and refused to let work become his life. Still, let's not get too depressed yet. We won't know anything for definite until the end of next week."

"But what will we do for money?"

Rosie hugged her daughter. "We'll be fine. If the worst happens, he'll get redundancy pay and he's bound to get another job. Besides we have no mortgage because of this place. Your great-uncle John had no money to leave, but these two houses must be worth a fair bit. Dad was really lucky inheriting them, but then he was the only one who bothered to visit Uncle John in that hospital."

Merryn wanted to ask her mum more about the strange uncle John. He had only figured in their lives these past three years. Prior to that, they did not know he even existed. Up until then, their extended family consisted only of a great aunt on her mother's side who lived in Bury St Edmunds with her revolting daughter. But out of the blue, a care worker at the hospital tracked Matt down explaining that his patient wanted to contact his family and make amends.

Uncle John had been in and out of psychiatric hospitals for most of his sixty-seven year life. His condition presented no physical danger to anyone but his constant talking could have bored the most patient person to death. He would ramble on and on about how his ancestors could not be blamed for their actions, they had no choice. The phrases, "he was doing what had to be done to rid the world of evil" and "it was cleansing" were his favourites. The professionals tried to analyse him, to discover what he was talking about, to reassure him. However, they failed so many times that they soon turned their attention to keeping him as comfortable and safe as they were able. They were not too successful at that either.

Bruises and cuts would often appear all over his body, but he denied all accusations of self-harming. Instead, Uncle John wailed that avenging spirits were punishing him; that he was being visited in the dark hours and beaten by his ancestor's victims. To the experts, he was a severely deluded man who was a danger to himself. To an onlooker, he was a rambling lunatic who was stuck way in the distant past.

By the time Matt reached him, Uncle John had developed a new trick. He would stand in the middle of the lounge and talk at whoever was unlucky enough to be in there. He told his audience that they had to look out for imps because imps were not to be trusted. He warned them of the punishments should they fall under the spell of an imp - the watching, being 'swum' and walking. He declared that these were not tortures, merely a necessity of a trial.

Luckily, anyone who was either too slow or not astute enough to run when they saw John coming, was probably not of the right frame of mind to be affected by his ranting. Nurses listened with half an ear then joked about what films he must have watched as a child. As his obsessive ranting escalated, he began calling for Matthew. He needed Matthew with him to prove that he was right. Matthew was the same as him – he was the only one who could help. Matthew could save him. Matthew knew how to help.

What else was the psychiatric staff meant to think? A lot of research uncovered a nephew called Matthew, and they assumed that he must have been the 'Matthew' from the ramblings. They knew that John's physical health was failing as rapidly as his mental state, so they acted in the best interests of their patient.

Delighted to find a living family member outside his own house, Matt visited his incoherent uncle whenever possible. Before his first visit, he imagined a joyful reunion, a sharing of memories, an understanding of his family history. What he had not expected was the hunched up, wizened creature who looked double his age. And he had not been prepared for the eyes. Matt often heard the expression about someone's eyes being haunted, but he assumed that was literary licence.

Uncle John's eyes were haunted. They darted around the room as though searching for an invisible threat, and they were filled with abject terror. The only time Matt managed to make eye contact made him wish he hadn't. He was staring at someone who had seen too much and was waiting for something much worse.

"Hello, Uncle John. It's me, Matthew," Matt whispered the first time he saw him. "Your nephew."

The old head creaked around and Matt felt himself being studied intently. After a full two minutes of silent investigation, these words were spoken in a clear, calm voice; "You are not Matthew."

Matt felt crushed with disappointment, but he felt a reassuring hand on his shoulder. "Don't worry. It's part of his condition. He barely remembers us and we see him nearly every day."

Over time, Matt felt less upset at not being recognised, and soon he did not care when his uncle declared, "You are not Matthew." He continued to do his duty out of familial love right until the day he arrived to be told that Uncle John had just died.

They said it was peaceful, that John fell asleep an hour earlier and slipped away gently. They did not tell Matthew that seconds before the end, the old man screamed in agony. His body had twisted and contorted as though something was burning his skin and his final words came out in a pitiful sob; "They're here for me."

Only Matt, his family and some of the carers from the hospital attended the funeral. Everyone commented on what a lovely send-off it was, but Matt merely shrugged and said that John deserved a dignified end despite the indignity of his life. Then he reaped a reward he neither demanded nor expected. Being the only living family member, he inherited his uncle's property.

But how would Matt have felt if he realised that he was indeed the wrong Matthew? His Uncle was calling for a man that had been dead for three hundred and fifty years – a man called Matthew Hopkins.

4

The watcher knew that she was asleep. She knew that she was dreaming, but it was so real. She was there; she was watching the action just as though it was street theatre and she was in the front row. This was more than that, though. Not only was she in a time gone by, with old cottages and greenery as far as the eye could see; a time that had no basis in her imagination or experience. But this felt like real life, and the watcher was on the outside looking in.

There would not be much food in the cupboards this winter, the old woman thought as she looked in despair at the pathetically wilted leaves in the vegetable patch. At least her land would be harvested, she gloated, looking at the crops in the fields to the back of her land that were dying from neglect. She sighed. If only life was easier.

It was not easy for anyone except for the rich. Stocks of food and fuel were running desperately low because there was no-one left to keep them going; all the able men were off fighting the war between the King and parliament. The old, the infirm and the women were left behind to tend the land and keep life going. What a mistake that was. Even their precious churches were suffering. Rumour, distrust and fingers of blame had left the church open to a take over by the Puritans. The churches were stripped of anything ornate or non-essential, and celebrations of any type were denounced as superstitious. Worship was no longer an act of celebration and pleasure; such ideas of fun were a sin. It was a terrible time of distrust and abstention.

She was old enough to remember the years before the troubles; when there had been enough food to go round, then a bit more. When the church had been a welcoming place of sanctuary. She and her husband spent their days working on the fields, and their evenings enjoying each other's company. Life had been good.

There had never been any children to brighten their lives. In those times, Alice Wright merely believed that she was one of the unlucky ones; now she knew that God was punishing her. She was being punished for going into that field with her brother and that boy. It hadn't been her fault, though. She had been enticed by the money, not by what he asked her to do. And she did not even do what he wanted; at least not everything. She showed him what he wanted to see, she let him touch, but nothing more. She was not wicked, just a hungry, foolish child. He paid her well, and her family ate heartily that evening.

She refused to waste her time on gossip but the village women whispered too loudly. Did they really think that she did not know what they said about her now? They muttered about witches and stopped as soon as she came near. All those pointed fingers talking about signs. Signs? What signs? All that nonsense about extra teats. Pah! She was an old woman - threescore and ten nearly. What did they expect of her? Everyone knew that your skin got loose and you grew a few warts.

So what if she talked to her cat? Snowbell did not answer her back; Snowbell did not look at her as if she had lost her senses; Snowbell was her true and only friend in this town of gossiping harridans. Alice scoffed at the idiocy of the so-called Puritans who called her cat an imp. An imp was a spirit of the devil, not a fat, white, lazy ball of ragged fur.

Her neighbour, Anne, was another of their victims. She lived in the cottage attached to her own, but they rarely spoke. Alice was wary of the woman's moods as they swung more powerfully than the church bells. Anne had been so helpful when Alice's husband died. She prepared the funeral meats, and she silenced the voices that declared Mr Wright's death by drowning was the result of too much ale.

There was another side to Anne though. The barbed comments that came out of nowhere, cut deeply and were absolutely unjustified. The way she screeched at people who strayed too close to her gardens as they left The Assembly Room and headed for the field. The public announcement that she had shut her cat up behind her wall to keep the witches away. It took weeks of sleepless nights until the wailing stopped.

Behind her facade of ignoring the village gossips, Alice was very scared of their power. There was talk of witch hunters cleansing this very county of evil; all in the name of the Puritan God. Witches had been discovered in Hadleigh, Lavenham and Bramford – named, tried and hanged. It was said that the witch finders were getting closer. Would they come here? If so, what would they discover here in Hitcham?

What could they discover? Hitcham was a God-fearing town that embraced the new religion and lost its men folk in the name of politics. There was nothing here; just a group of men too old, too lazy or unfit to fight and a horde of hysterical women, concocting rumours about people they did not like.

Yet the anxiety continued. Alice walked away from her failed vegetable patch towards The Assembly Room. It was her duty to clean the building every time the community had used it. It was not a duty of love or enjoyment but she did her job without a grumble. It helped fill her hours.

Today, the cold, unwelcoming building felt colder than ever and she felt a distinct chill travel down her spine. Dismissing her fears as an old woman's silliness, Alice went to look out of the window. The previous day, she had imagined that she saw a face looking at her from the outside. It was the face of a young lady, though she seemed somewhat wrong and out of her true place. Alice blinked and the illusion vanished. Today, she could see nothing there but she still had a strong feeling that she was being watched. With a shiver, she turned back to her work although she could not shake the idea that someone had seen her looking through that window. "Stop being such a foolish old woman!" she chided herself. "You'll be taken away as a witch."

A fat, white, scruffy cat slinked through the doorway and began to wrap herself around her mistress's legs. "Oh, Snowbell, you imp!" Alice scolded. "You made me jump, you little minx. Was that you watching me out there? Have you been out finding your own supper again? Those poor wretched mice."

And so the monologue went on much to the delight of the group of women who happened to be passing. What more proof of witchcraft could they need? It was time to write the letter of invitation.

The watcher woke with a start, feeling disorientated and confused. Looking round, she saw her fireplace and felt her white cat snuggled on her feet. Everything was as it should be, except for an ominous nagging in her mind.

5

"You look exhausted, Merryn," Rosie observed. "Bad night?"

"I had a really weird dream, but I can't remember it all that well. It wasn't scary but it wasn't nice either. There was an old woman in it called Alice and she was worried about someone coming to her village. And it was ancient – like centuries ago. Sounds crazy, I know. I can't help it. Anyway, I'm going to be late. I'll see you later."

Merryn grabbed her school bag and dashed out of the door. She saw Jamie wave at her from the stop outside The Assembly Room, then made a point of walking hesitantly towards him.

In answer to his quizzical look, she asked, "Do we have to stand here? Would the bus still stop if we stood on the grassed bit?"

"We can try it if you like." He gave her a bit of a strange look but reached down for his bag. Without answering, Merryn walked ten paces away to the open greensward front of her garden.

"Are you scared of the ghosts of the Assembly Room?" Jamie teased. "It's meant to be haunted, you know."

"Haunted by what?" Merryn questioned hurriedly, her face turning pale.

"Oh, I don't know; I don't believe in all that rubbish. I think it's something to do with witches though, and the trials in the seventeenth century. You're doing history, aren't you? Ask the teacher. We're doing medieval witchcraft and he's an expert."

Jamie was right. Mr Carter was an expert. But even more than that, he was an amazing teacher. Everyone in the class hung onto his words – even the typical 'can't be bothered' students were asking questions and looking keen.

It seemed that while Matthew Hopkins is the name that most people remember, it was in fact his sidekick who cleansed the western side of the old Ipswich to Norwich road. Mr Hopkins remained on his native Eastern side.

Matthew Hopkins and his team of assistants started their tyranny in his home-town of Manningtree in 1645, extracting a confession out of a one-legged woman called Elizabeth Clarke. After making her walk non-stop for three days and nights, she confessed to having five 'imps' in the form of dogs and cats that helped her do the devil's work. She also implicated five other women, who gave the names of others. That was a pretty successful start to Hopkins' career: four died in prison and about nineteen were hanged. And he would have been paid well for his troubles.

He carried on doing his cleansing as far distant as Lowestoft and Aldeburgh, before arriving at Stowmarket. No one knew exactly how many of his tried witches died on the gallows, but he managed to get rid of eighteen of them in one day at the infamous August 27th trial of 1645 in Bury St Edmunds.

By the end of the lesson, Merryn's head was buzzing with facts and questions. Was this Matthew Hopkins anything to do with the Hitcham witches that Jamie had mentioned?

"Next week, class," Mr Carter announced over the chatter, "We will look at the route taken by Mr Hopkins' partner in crime – Mr John Stearne. Not related to you, Merryn, is he?"

That remark was meant to be flippant - a teacher's attempt at humour that elicited polite chuckles from polite students. But it set a far from flippant train of thought racing through Merryn's head. Could she be linked to the infamous John Stearne? It was not a common name, and her great-uncle was obsessed with witches. It had to be a coincidence, didn't it? For some reason that she would not have been able to explain, however, it did not feel like it.

"What happened to you in there?" Jamie asked as they sat on the bus home. "I thought you were going to throw up! Mr Carter was only joking, you know. It would be a laugh if he was your great-great-great-great-great-granddad, wouldn't it?"

"Yeah, hilarious!"

"I'm sorry. Don't be so moody."

"Look, I'm sorry," Merryn said. "I'm still stressed from all the moving stuff. Tell me about the ghosts of The Assembly Room."

"There aren't any ghosts really. Some people reckon they've heard noises like moaning and all that. You know, ghost-story noises. And other people say they've gone in there and felt things touch them on the back. There's so much junk in there, they probably just walked into something. And then there's the karma freaks, going on about the vibes of the place. It stinks just like old places do and it's decaying because some rodent will have died in there. There you go – no ghosts."

Satisfied with his argument, Jamie turned to talk to the boy sitting behind him leaving Merryn to her thoughts. He must be right. Ghosts had been proven so many times to be figments of the imagination; there were always plausible scientific explanations for their so-called hauntings. Merryn always believed herself to be on the side of science. However, that same instinct that whispered to her about John Stearne was now telling her to listen to her heart.

As the bus drew up to their cluster of houses, Merryn stood up in the aisle and glanced across at The Assembly Room. Once again, a flicker of movement caught her eye, and she peered at one of the windows next to the door. This time it was unmistakable. There was a face there. It was an old woman and she seemed to be staring straight at Merryn. The more Merryn stared, however, the more she realised that the woman was not looking at her, just gazing out at nothing in particular. The face was familiar, but Merryn could not place where she had seen it before.

"Get a move on, slowcoach!" Jamie prodded her in the back and she had to move on. Once they were off the bus, Merryn looked at the window again. But there was nothing there. How could there be? There was no glass at the window – merely that ragged patchwork of thick cardboard and wood. There was no way anyone could see anything at that window frame.

6

"Any news on Dad's job yet?" Merryn asked Rosie as she walked into the kitchen.

"It's not good, I'm afraid," her mum answered. "They haven't said anything for definite, but your dad hasn't been given anything new to do since Monday. And you know how much they used to pile work up on him. Can we change the subject? How was your day?"

With a renewed enthusiasm, and memories of ghostly faces filed in a subconscious part of her mind, Merryn told her fascinated mum all about their witchy heritage. Then she broached the subject of the family link with John Stearne.

"You know," murmured her mother, "Your dad mentioned some sort of rumour about being distantly related to some villain in the past. But no one knew much about it, and there wasn't really anyone to ask anyway. We do have the same surname so I suppose there might be a link somewhere. I wouldn't worry about it though – everyone has a skeleton in a cupboard somewhere. Besides, three hundred and fifty years is a long time to dilute any evil that was in the Stearne genetics."

Merryn left Rosie to follow her incredibly detailed instructions about lighting the stove and went to her room. Snowdrop was still in her cat basket. She would only leave to use her litter tray; even her meals had to be given in the basket. As had become the norm, Snowdrop started purring loudly as soon as Merryn stroked her, but she would not come out.

Merryn was losing patience with her cat, so she decided to try a new idea. She picked up the basket and carried it into her parents' bedroom. Immediately, Snowdrop started growling and hissing. Telling the wailing beast to keep quiet, Merryn put the basket on the floor between the window and the hearth.

As she opened the door of the basket, Snowdrop shot out and stood in front of the boarded-up fireplace. She sniffed at the wood then jumped away as though she had felt an electric shock. Next, the cat held out a tentative paw and began patting at the board. The patting became quicker and Snowdrop put her weight on her back paws so that she could alternate which front paw she was using. Merryn heard a growl coming from the animal and was shocked to see that the pawing had become ever more frantic scratching. The more Snowdrop scratched, the more she spat and the more her fur stood on end. Merryn was getting so scared by her cat's manic behaviour that she yelled for help.

"Mum! Mum! Come here quick! It's Snowdrop!"

Rosie was upstairs in seconds and watched with a mixture of bemusement and fear as the feline now started trying to bite at the wood.

"Have you tried pulling her away?" asked Rosie.

Merryn went to grab Snowdrop by the waist but in a flash, a paw-full of sharp claws cut deeply into her hand drawing blood from each wound. "What are we going to do? We can't just leave her," wailed Merryn. "She's hurting herself. There's blood on the wood."

Rosie crouched down and wrapped a handkerchief around her daughter's hand. "There must be something behind there. Why else would she be going so mad? I'll have a look. It's probably a mouse or something, and it'll be long gone before I get this off."

As soon as Rosie started to tug at the wood, Snowdrop calmed down. Her fur was still up on end and she was still growling deep in the back of her throat. But she seemed content to watch and let someone help her.

It took a lot of leverage with a screwdriver that Matt had left on the mantelpiece, and even more elbow grease to release the wood. "This has been here for a long time," muttered Rosie as she cursed the cat. "I'm not even sure what it has been sealed with."

When it came away suddenly, both mother and daughter wished it had stayed put. They fell backwards onto the floor, coughing, spluttering and choking. At least a couple of hundred years' worth of dust and debris from the chimney floated through the air seeking a surface to cover. Snowdrop chose that moment to run howling from the room.

The true horror came when the dust cloud settled and the Stearne women had wiped the grit and soot from their eyes. Most of the rubble in the fireplace lay relatively flat but just away from the centre was a raised heap. It looked as though there was something beneath it. Rosie and Merryn began to move aside the bricks and debris, sweeping away the soot with their bare hands.

"Mum, I can feel something." With the care of an archaeologist, Merryn continued excavating until the object was revealed. Without realising what she was holding, she picked it up and held it out in proud display.

Then she looked, she realised, she dropped it and she screamed. Rosie did not scream but she looked on in horror. Lying on the floor in front of them was the mummified remains of a cat.

Half an hour later, with the initial horror behind them, Merryn and her mother were sitting at the kitchen table with the cat in front of them. Rosie had looked at the mummified remains and could see no obvious signs of injury on the corpse. The skeleton was fully intact and some skin was still covering the bones, although the fur was gone. The worst thing was the mouth, which was open wide in mid-howl.

Rosie and Merryn looked with pity at the poor creature, and tried to guess what could have happened. The screaming mouth suggested that the animal had died in pain; the tensed limbs and clenched claws backed up this idea. However that did not explain how it got to be there in the first place. In the end, they came to the horrible theory that the animal had been blocked up while still alive. Surely no one would do that, would they? Rosie and Merryn decided to use the power of the Internet to see if they could get any information.

After trawling through more than a few dead ends, Merryn came up with the possible answer. "It looks like it's to do with witchcraft," she said. "Apparently, people would brick up a living cat behind their walls, or in their chimneys, to keep witches out. They thought that a witch wouldn't want to go into a house with a cat in it. Oh my God. That is so disgusting."

"These houses are pretty old – round about sixteenth century, so that would fit in with the witchcraft stuff that you were talking about earlier. But that poor little thing could have been put in there at any time. It doesn't prove anything," responded Rosie.

"It proves there were witches around here."

"No, Merryn. Don't get all panicky. It only proves that whoever lived here used to be terrified of witches. Even now, we have superstitions and things to keep us safe: like St Christopher chains for safe journeys, dream catchers for nightmares."

But Merryn could not keep the panic away. "But blocking a cat behind a wall is just evil. We've been sleeping in the house with a mummified cat. In a house where there used to be witches. I hate this place and I want to go home!"

Merryn ran upstairs and slammed her bedroom door, only to see Snowdrop stretched out on her bed, cleaning her paws and purring loudly. If cats could smile, Snowdrop would be smirking.

7

The watcher saw them coming for the old woman. She knew they would. Alice too had known it. That crowd of gossiping hags had too much time and idle tongues. If their men folk were here and not away fighting the battles, they would not let their women make evil chatter. They would not let them bring shame like that.

The previous day, he had ridden into their quiet lives with his group of assistants, bringing chaos disguised as authority in his stead. He was dressed as a gentleman, with his rich, pressed garments, but his manner was such an obvious pretence. Fancy clothes could not hide the working-man beneath. He greeted everyone he saw with jolly humility, thanking them for allowing him to visit such a wonderful town. Though he never removed his hat; he just tipped the rim a little.

In a place where gossip controls daily life, it did not take long for most of the townsfolk to be out of their houses, waiting to catch a glimpse of the enigmatic stranger. Therefore, his announcement of a meeting at The Assembly Room that evening was heard by most. Those who did not hear directly were soon told. No one asked the purpose of the meeting - they already knew. This was the man they had called for, the man who would help rid their town of witches.

All the townsfolk, including Alice, attended the meeting. The watcher was standing at an ethereal distance, not part of their number but a witness to everything. Try as she might, she could not see the stranger's features beneath his enormous rimmed hat.

The watcher heard the stranger introduce himself as John Stearne and listened to him throw compliment after compliment on the townsfolk. He extolled the Puritanical excellence of their church, the wondrously strong sense of the community and the feeling of overwhelming good amongst most of the inhabitants.

Basking in the glory of their virtuosity, the Hitcham townsfolk barely noticed when he started to talk like a preacher. He told them that this country would not escape from the fighting and the famine until it was cleansed of evil. Their fathers, husbands, brothers and sons would not come home until the wicked seeds within their midst had gone. All their sacrifice to create the new religion would have been for nothing as there were forces at work desperate to undo all their good work.

He appealed to their fears and their anger. They wanted someone to blame for their days of fasting and their hunger. They needed a scapegoat for the way their churches had been looted. They wanted a person to accuse for the deaths of their families in the troubles. He was more than happy to find a victim for them. In fact, he told them it was his duty.

It did not take long for him to get most of the village on his side. He showed them the alternatives, though he was careful not to mention the word 'witch'. He could not allow himself to be accused of leading the accusations, just in case his practice was ever brought into question. However, it never took long for his audience to whisper the word themselves, and then hysteria spread like fire.

"Do you want a life with no fear where you can trust all your neighbours? Of course you do! Do you want a community that follows the way of the Lord? Of course you do! Do you want a clean village where the devil is scared to tread? Of course you do! I am here to help you! I can rid the evil from your community. I can cleanse your village. You will be able to live again as God serving believers, with none of Satan's helpers muddying your waters. Your homes will once again be free from the threat of evil that has pulled our country into the mire in which it is now stuck."

And on he went, stirring the listeners into action. He planted the seeds of doubt in their minds and made them look again at the members of their village that they did not really like. He assured his listeners that no one was to be scared of laying blame; it was their duty to the country and to the church. If the accusations were found to be true, then the accuser would be doing a honourable service to their country. If the accusations were unfounded, then justice would still have been served and the accusers would have nothing to fear.

A few villagers mumbled dissent at the witch-hunter. They were not believers in the witchcraft scourge, but they knew better than to say anything. Showing opposition to the trials could well open up accusations of devil worshipping. But this same crowd of non-conformists did openly question the cost of cleansing.

The stranger's answer was as smooth as the rest of his arguments. "As I said to you, the fee of £2 is nothing compared to the cost of the consequences. What will happen to you if you allow the devil to run free in your lives? Can you put a price on your soul? In these terrible times, you have a duty to protect the values of your country. You have a duty to protect your family. You have a duty to God."

Now, the watcher saw the stranger and his entourage walk up the path to Alice Wright's front door. What had she ever done to anyone? She was old, her skin was becoming blotched and her hair was falling out. She was grumpy and she talked to her cat. She walked with a limp, having one leg slightly shorter than the other and her shoulders were hunched through age.

The group of upwards of forty women who gathered outside The Assembly Room, hated Alice. Between their braying for justice, they scared each other with tales of how the old woman had bewitched a cow so it would not produce milk, and the horse that suddenly fell lame. They could not find a true, substantiated grievance about the woman but that did not upset anyone – they had enough tales in their own minds. Perhaps Alice's only crime against these women was that she shunned their company. She did not care what people thought of her. She did not need their acceptance.

The witch-finder knocked at her door followed by his group of assistants. Quite clearly enjoying his task, John Stearne delivered his speech. "Goodwife Wright, I am sent as an ambassador of God to do the work of the Lord and cleanse our society of witches. You are accused of witchcraft. As a child, you did consort with the devil and now you keep an imp in the form of a white cat to do the devil's work."

Alice was led from her house with her head bowed and she shuffled the short distance to The Assembly Room. She was not protesting loudly but her mutters could be heard as she pointed to the gang of onlookers screeching for justice. "I am no witch. I do not have an imp. She is my pet. They'll be the witches you are after." That made the gossiping gaggle gasp in horror and they huddled together as though to shield themselves from her threatening presence. Hysteria had well and truly found a new home.

The show was all over and now the interrogation was about to take place behind the closed doors of The Assembly Room.

Merryn woke up with a scream trying to escape from her parched throat. The house in her dream was her house. And the old woman in her dream was the face she had seen in the window of The Assembly Room.

8

Merryn sat at the kitchen table the following morning with her head on her arms.

"Bad night?" asked her dad as he walked into the room.

"What are you doing here?" Merryn was surprised to see him in jeans and a t-shirt, and at home on a Friday.

"It's D-Day for my job. They're having a board meeting today, and the people who it really affects are not invited – as usual. So I may never be going back to London."

Merryn stood up and hugged her dad. "We'll be okay, sweetheart," he mumbled. "It's only a silly old job. I've got everything I need here: a beautiful daughter, a lovely wife, a house to restore and a haunted building to play in."

"Will you stop going on about it being haunted!" yelled Merryn.

"I was only joking! Don't panic! Just because the place looks such a mess doesn't mean it's haunted. Besides there's no such thing as ghosts; that's what you always told me when I had nightmares after reading Stephen King. Remember?"

"I've changed my mind," Merryn said as she slammed the front door and went to catch the school bus.

Jamie had remembered the new bus stop arrangement and was sitting on a large hold all. "Cricket tournament today," he answered to her unspoken question. "You need to get some 'Nytol' or something – you look shattered."

"Thanks a lot," Merryn mumbled. "Bad dreams, that's all."

Jamie rabbited on about how it must be something to do with settling in and getting used to the clean country air. Merryn let him go on so she did not have to tell him about the dreams. He would think she was absolutely nuts, and she did not want him to think that. It was quite awkward actually because, in her head, she was determined that he was just a friend. But in her heart, she couldn't help fancying her friend.

They managed to get the back seat, and as the bus drove away, Jamie turned round. "Hey, why is your dad going into The Assembly Room?" he asked.

Merryn spun round in horror. She wanted to yell at his disappearing back to keep out, that he was in danger, but it was too late. Once again, she had a gut feeling that something was very wrong and she could do nothing about it.

Matt had not been able to stop picturing the look on Merryn's face as he joked about The Assembly Room. She was the one who could watch 'Paranormal Activity' and yawn. She would study so-called phenomena on photographs and point out the errors. Merryn did not do hysteria – it was not in her nature. So surely she did not really believe that this old building was haunted? Mind you, it did look a bit creepy, and it was the sort of place that would be the star of a TV paranormal show. With too much thinking time on his hands, Matt decided to go and investigate - just to put his daughter's mind at rest.

On a large, rusty key ring, Matt tried about two thirds of the keys until he found the right one. This was really ghost story-ish. The key was large and Gothic looking. It opened a lock that was little more than a hole in the wooden door with a circular latch above.

The door creaked open as Matt pushed. He was hit by a smell of damp, dust and decay, and he had to cover his nose and mouth with the bottom of his t-shirt. With his other hand, he swung the torch round illuminating thousands of spider webs and many pieces of old furniture.

Brushing a large, hairy spider from his shoulder, Matt felt extremely glad that Merryn was not with him. He may not have believed in ghosts but it was spooky in here. The temperature had plummeted as soon as he stepped over the threshold, and the air felt thick enough to touch. It was hardly welcoming. Had he been less sceptical, Matt would have described the atmosphere as hostile. But how could that have been possible in an empty building?

Matt refused to be beaten by superstition so he carried on exploring. There were a lot of wooden chairs, which seemed to be in good condition except for the dirt. There was also a very long wooden table that he decided would work well as a dining table in the other house. Several other smaller tables were dotted around. Tucked in the corner was a thick, long piece of rope – home now to dust and arachnids.

He had just picked up a handful of ancient tools and a few old books when Rosie shouted his name. Matt left the building hurriedly, being too concerned about his wife's summons to notice that the door he had left open was slowly creaking shut behind him. Had he turned, he would have noticed the outline of a man pushing the door shut and the face of an old woman staring at him with pleading in her eyes.

Rosie called him in to take a telephone call. As she watched his changing expressions, she knew that it was the news he had expected and it was not good. He put the phone down and sat at the kitchen table. Rosie busied herself with making a pot of tea, then they sat and talked.

"That's it then. I'm now unemployed. It could have been worse," he said. "After all, I will get redundancy pay - they're going to give me the figure soon. I won't be paying those extortionate fares any more, or getting stuck in overheated trains for hours on end whenever they feel like running late. Plus I'll be at home more. Not sure if you and Merryn will approve of that though!" Matt stopped to finish his tea, then let silence fill the air between them for a full minute.

"Seriously, Rosie. What are we going to do when the money runs out? I'm forty-two, I've been with the same company for twenty years, my job is so specialised that no one else really needs people like me. Plus there are no jobs in what I have experience in, especially not around here. Suffolk is hardly a Mecca of employment for a computer geek like me who specialises in software for large corporate banks."

Matt was getting so morose that Rosie decided to offer her thoughts. "How about doing up that house next door and then we can sell it? Then we can work on The Assembly Room and turn it into some sort of business. I don't know - a tearoom or something. I can fit my accountancy studying in around running that."

"Believe me, you wouldn't want to have a cup of tea in there," was Matt's reply. "But I agree with you about the house next door.

Maybe me and you could do that together. We'll call ourselves 'Stearne Renovations'. Perhaps not! It doesn't sound too inviting, does it?"

With his mood temporarily lifted, Matt and Rosie discussed their plans and began to tenuously look forward to their future. If only they could have known what affect such future plans would have on the past.

9

The following week, Merryn was sitting on the school field with Jamie's group of friends. There were seven of them usually, counting herself and Jamie. Rob and Ed were twins in birth only – not in looks or personality. Edward got the looks and charisma while Rob made do with the brains. Ed was tall, one of the top ten fittest boys in school (apparently) and possessed an amazing sense of humour; Rob was short, slightly dumpy and had the rare gift of empathy. Marcus tagged along as Ed's sidekick, usually inheriting the good-looking girl's friend. He did not make the top ten list but he was not too far off. The female element of the group consisted of Maria and Lily. Of their group, only Merryn and Jamie lived in Hitcham, with Rob hailing from the neighbouring town of Bildeston and the others all coming from Hadleigh.

Merryn was nearly at the point of calling them 'her' friends, but she did not want to get too cosy just yet. It seemed too good to be true: an okay school and some great new friends. Plus there was Jamie.

Every minute she spent with him aggravated the head versus heart dilemma. He was such a fantastic friend that she did not want to spoil that with romance. Everyone said that you should never let your guy-mate become your boyfriend because of the post-splitting up consequences. But she knew that she wanted so much more. She wanted the closeness, the contact and the cuddles that only a boyfriend could give. Occasionally, Merryn caught Jamie looking at her and he had always turned away quickly. She did allow her heart to have the odd little flutter and imagine that he felt the way that she did. Then she let her sensible head speak reason and explain that no one so gorgeous could possibly fancy her. They were mates – end of.

As well as socially, life had also got easier at home. With her dad's new self-employed status, he was totally unstressed. She loved having him around, even if he was constantly speaking about his renovation ideas. She had slept soundly for six nights and addressed her fear of The Assembly Room by ignoring it. Life was good and Merryn was loving it.

Rob, Jamie's best friend since primary school, was sitting next to Merryn, complaining about the history project that Mr Carter had set. Each pupil was to produce a 1,500 word essay on the witchcraft trials of 1645. Interesting - maybe; hard work – definitely!

"Can I get a look around your Assembly Room?" Rob asked Merryn suddenly.

The colour drained away from her face as she turned to him. "What did you say?"

"The Assembly Room. It is yours, isn't it? Can I get a look inside for the project?"

Merryn felt her hands become sticky and fear tickled her neck. "What do you want to go in there for?"

"Because of the witchcraft trials and everything," Rob said.

All of a sudden, the rest of the group had gone silent and were listening intently. "You did know, didn't you?" interjected Maria, a tall, dark-haired girl who had inherited her Philippine mother's beauty and poise, and her French father's analytical brain.

Merryn intercepted a warning look sent from Jamie to Maria, and glared at the boy. "Tell me," she said. Silence plummeted on the group as everyone looked at everyone else for a get out clause. Eventually, Maria took pity on Merryn and took a deep breath.

"Okay. You know those women that Mr Carter was on about? The ones from Hitcham who were tried by John Stearne? Well, there's no evidence to prove it, but they think that the trials were done at The Assembly Room."

"If there's no evidence, how do they know?" Merryn argued.

"Because…" said Lily, who was normally the quiet one; the one they relied on to bring reason back into any situation. "There is nowhere else it could have been. Hitcham was a large village then, maybe a town, but it was still just a load of houses, a pub and The Assembly Room. He wouldn't have done the trials in the pub because there wasn't the space, and The Assembly Room was the only other place big enough."

"No way!" Merryn interrupted. "That's just wrong. It must be. Anyway, The Assembly Room isn't old enough!" Jamie heard the hopeful triumph in her last words and saw the anxiety building in her eyes.

Taking a deep breath, Jamie mimicked the tone he had heard his mother use on the countless occasions when she was trying to reassure him that everything would be all right, knowing full well that it wouldn't. "The Assembly Room keeps getting rebuilt. It's burnt down a few times, but there's always been something there. It's been used for all sorts of stuff too. It doesn't mean anything though. Just because they might have done the trials there doesn't mean there's anything there now."

At the turn in the conversation, Ed suddenly perked up. "Hey, you don't reckon it's haunted, do you? That would be so cool living next to a haunted house. Hey, Merryn. Is it haunted? Have you seen anything?"

Rob started telling his twin to stop talking, but Ed was too carried away. "I've got a great idea. Why don't we spend a night in The Assembly Room? Then we can write it up for our projects. Call it 'A Night with the Witches' or 'The Hitcham Witch Project'. What do you reckon?"

Marcus and Ed started eagerly planning their adventure without waiting for permission. Even Maria and Lily were swept along in the planning. They were discussing what food they could bring and whether anyone had something to play a DVD on. Meanwhile Merryn sank further into the grass as the panic flooding over her threatened to drown her. She barely noticed when an arm was put around her and subconsciously she nestled into the embrace. She felt safe, warm and cosy.

"Are you okay, Merryn?" a soft voice whispered in her ear. She realised it was Jamie and quickly pulled herself away.

Blushing furiously, she mumbled something but kept her eyes firmly fixed on the grass. She did not see the hurt look in Jamie's eyes as she distanced herself from him.

"Look, you lot," Jamie said brusquely. "Don't you think you're getting a bit carried away? That place is falling to pieces and I know for a fact that Merryn's dad wouldn't let you sleep there. Health and safety, and all that! Maybe you'd be allowed to visit, but that's up to Merryn."

Merryn knew she had to say something but she couldn't. She felt so embarrassed. Jamie had only been comforting her, but she enjoyed it. He must have thought she was a real idiot cuddling into him. She really had blown her chances with him – totally and utterly. The bell for afternoon lessons rang and Merryn was saved not only from the constant badgering from Ed and Marcus about the sleepover, but also from her own stupidity.

That afternoon's lessons dragged on and Merryn did not see Jamie again. By the time the bus came, she managed to work out a way of breaking the ice and maybe diffusing the situation. She had forgotten that she would not see Jamie on the way home because of another cricket match.

As the bus pulled up at The Assembly Room, Merryn's mind had been on Jamie. However, as she crossed the road those thoughts vanished. She found herself standing directly outside the entrance to the building and the door was slightly ajar showing nothing except pitch-blackness. "Dad!" she called. "Dad! Are you in there?"

There was no answer, although the door creaked open a couple more centimetres. "Dad! Is that you? Answer me. It's not funny!" cried Merryn, frozen to the spot with terror.

The door started to open again when a dark figure appeared out of the blackness. It was impossible to make out any features, but Merryn knew that it was a man. He appeared to be wearing a hat, and riding boots. Merryn felt his eyes studying her mockingly. She saw him raise his hand towards the door and push it shut slowly. As he pushed, she heard the voice of a woman scream out, "Help me! Please help me!"

The door clicked shut and there was a sudden movement at the window. Merryn heard a banging at the frame, and the same voice screaming, "You have to help me!" She saw that face again; the same woman – old, frail, and terrified with tears streaming down her cheeks. She was looking straight at Merryn this time, with desperation in her eyes. Then suddenly she was gone, as though she had been dragged away.

With the spell broken, Merryn ran to her house and tore straight up the stairs to her bedroom, slamming the door and sitting with her back against it. Once she stopped crying and shaking, she remembered where she had seen that old woman before; it was the accused witch from her dreams.

10

The watcher was inside a dark building looking at a group of four people standing around a forlorn, old woman who was tied to a wooden chair.

"Have you examined her, Goody Phillips?" the watcher heard the man ask. The stranger wore the clothes of a gentleman but did not have the bearing. She knew him for what he was – a common crook.

"I have searched her everywhere, Master Stearne, but I can find only one mark under her arm and I do not believe it will work." Goodwife Phillips looked down at the old woman with a mixture of scorn and disgust in her eyes. She was a plump woman with a face lined by frowns and such an aura of aggression that the watcher doubted anyone would dare to argue with her.

She had seen Goody Phillips and her helper, Goody Mills, search the wretched woman for evidence of devil's marks, spots or blotches of irregular colour on her skin. They made her strip; they would have shaved her hair except that the old lady had so little hair on her head. But their investigation was in vain. There were no moles or birthmarks large enough for a successful pricking and they could not do the pricking in public unless they were sure it would be successful.

"We will use that devil's mark," announced John Stearne. He lifted the frail woman's left arm and searched for the tiny liver coloured spot. It took him a while to find it, and he was disappointed by its size. He flung back the woman's arm as if it was a rag to be thrown away.

Tied to the chair by her legs and subjected to hours of questions, Alice Wright did not protest. When the witch-hunters' assistants searched even the most intimate parts of her body for signs of possession, Alice's eyes burned with humiliation but her *body lacked the strength to fight back, and her mind was losing the will to defend her character.*

"That mark will bleed," Goody Phillips reiterated, "we cannot use it."

"It will not bleed," Master Stearne's voice became sinister and he addressed his answer to the old woman's face. "However, to be safe, we will do the pricking here, not out there. I will go and talk to the crowd."

The man went to the front door of The Assembly Room, and opened it with a flourish. There was a group of about thirty people waiting expectantly. Most of them were women, although there were some children and a few of the older men of the town. They fell silent but they all craned their necks to try and take a glimpse into the blackness of the room.

"We have found a mark of the devil!" he announced and the crowd cheered, before they started shouting to see the mark. Once more, John Stearne's deep voice quelled the melee. "This creature is so possessed by the devil that we are worried about your safety. Therefore we will do the pricking inside this building."

That caused a different reaction. The response was quieter as fear mixed with the blood lust, but one person could be heard clearly. "As an elder of our church, I would like to be present at the pricking so that I can prove to these people that justice is being done."

John Stearne glared at the middle-aged man. "Do you suggest that justice will not be done by myself and my assistants?"

"Not at all, Mr Stearne. But, as you know, most prickings are conducted in public and that is proof in itself. If you propose to do the pricking inside, you must have witnesses that are independent of your own group." Master Stirman was the man brave enough to stand up for the rights of the accused. Two other men, who had been connected with the church in the days before Puritanism, stood beside him to offer their support. They too were as sceptical about the persecution of so-called witches.

John Stearne weighed up the possibilities. It was true: prickings were usually a public spectacle but he knew that this one might be risky. And he needed to keep the locals on his side. Better to have three witnesses than thirty. Besides, he had the tools to do the job properly. *"Very well, you gentlemen may witness the proceedings and report back to your townsfolk. Although I ask you to take great care when you join us. From what we have witnessed in this room, I cannot guarantee your safety."* That threat should scare anyone else who dared question him, he decided.

The crowd parted to allow the three well-dressed men into the building, then they fell back to whispering, questioning the bravery or folly of the witnesses.

"Fetch the pricking instruments, Goody Phillips," ordered the witch-pricker as he re-entered The Assembly Room, followed by Master Stirman and the two elders. *"You gentlemen stand there near the accused's left arm, but leave me room to move."*

Goody Phillips had heard the commotion outside and had prepared the instruments in advance. There were three dagger-like weapons, with ornate handles and long spikes at the end. She placed a fourth implement there, but this one was different. It was hollow inside the handle, so that when it was pressed against the skin, the blade would retract and the skin would not be pierced.

"The pricking will give proof of possession by the devil," Mr Stearne declared. *"Do you see this mark under her arm?"*

The men peered at the small mark on the old woman's skin. *"It is a mole, is it not? Or some form of wart?"* Master Stirman questioned.

"No, sir," came the reply. *"It is a mark of the devil. I will prick this mark and we will watch her reaction. If she bleeds and shows pain, then she is not a witch. However, if she does not bleed and feels no pain, then she is a witch. Goody Phillips? Goody Mills? Are you ready?"*

Goody Mills held up Alice Wright's arm as Goody Phillips passed the bodkin with the hollow handle. Behind them, the fourth member of the witch-hunter's group, Edward Parsley, prepared to record the outcome on an official looking pad. Alice started to thrash around in the chair as she saw the weapon come towards her, so Goody Phillips hastily tied the old woman's free arm to the chair.

With an exaggerated plea to God to show justice, John Stearne lowered the pricker onto the 'devil's mark' under Alice's arm. As *the point pressed against the hairs protruding from the blemish, the blade slid into the hilt. Alice Wright neither screamed, nor bled. "Gentlemen," the witch-finder declared to the witnesses. "The woman is a witch!"*

At this point, Alice screamed, "No! I am not a witch. Do it again! I am not a witch."

Suddenly, Mr Stirman grabbed a different bodkin from the collection left on the table by Goody Phillips. He stabbed that pricker into the wart before anyone could stop him.

Alice screamed in pain – a loud, piercing scream that made the crowd outside stop their mumblings. Blood trickled slowly but steadily from the wound as the gentleman held up the pricker and announced, "This woman is no witch. Release her."

At that moment, Merryn woke up screaming. A terrible pain throbbed just under her left arm as though she had been stabbed. She felt something wet and sticky, so she groped in the darkness to switch on her light. Her sheets were covered in blood that was coming from a small hole under her left arm.

11

"How did you say you did this?" asked Rosie the following morning as she bandaged Merryn's wounded arm.

"I've already said. I don't know. I must have knocked the top off a spot or something."

Rosie's response of, "It must have been a pretty big spot" just brought a glare. She had heard the screams in the early hours of the morning and had gone into her daughter's bedroom. But as soon as she stood in the girl's doorway, Merryn began to yell, "Get away from me! I'm not a witch! Go away! I'm not a witch!" Believing that her daughter was dreaming, Rosie walked away, knowing that there was nothing she could do to help. She had not noticed the bloodstained bedding.

As a child, Merryn suffered night terrors for a full week. She had screamed and grown more hysterical if her mother tried to cuddle her. Rosie was told that such fits were fairly common and would have no long-term side effects on the child, but that did not stop them being terrifying for the watcher. It was like watching someone possessed.

Last night had been a flashback to the terrors as Rosie stood helplessly in the doorway. The wailing, the thrashing and the yelling went on for well over an hour, until Merryn lapsed into a deep sleep with tears sliding down her cheeks. At this point, Rosie had gone over and kissed her daughter on the forehead, then returned to bed. She could sleep no more that night as she was waiting for a repeat performance.

"Do you want to take a spare pad and bandage to school just in case it starts bleeding again?" Rosie offered as Merryn picked up her school bag.

"Mum! Will you stop fussing?" was the reply she got before the door slammed. What had happened to her easy-going, friendly child? Merryn was turning into the terrible teenager Rosie had been warned about.

Matt came into the kitchen, covered in dust but still smiling. "What have you done to Merryn? She is in a right grump."

"Don't ask," groaned Rosie. "I suppose you'll be wanting a cup of tea before you get back to work?"

"In a minute. I want to show you something first. Are you busy?"

Rosie followed Matt across the path to their neighbouring house. It was looking better already. There was glass in the windows, and the rubble had found a new home in an ever-growing heap in the back garden. The floors were still sloping and there were holes in the ceilings, but the potential was more obvious.

"Look over here," instructed Matt. He was standing just inside the kitchen. His first discovery had appeared when the hideous false walling that covered almost every vertical surface was removed. Beautiful oak beams, miraculously uninhabited by woodworm, now stood proud on every wall. His subsequent discoveries, however, had been far more interesting.

When Matt pulled away the latest piece of wood, he found a stone bottle that was about ten centimetres high with the face of a bearded man carved on the neck and the front. An ancient cork was wedged in the opening. He put the bottle to one side, however, when he found the shoes on a ledge just up the chimney.

They were withered and ancient, and he had to hold them carefully so that they did not fall to pieces. There were two shoes but they were quite clearly not a pair. One was very little, and it was the size of a young child's shoe. The other seemed larger, possibly that of a small adult. They were made of leather with holes for laces. Many different feet had obviously worn them as there were several outlines of toe imprints, and there was evidence that the shoe had been repaired numerous times.

"Well?" Matt smiled.

"Very interesting but very disgusting," replied Rosie. "Do you think they've got anything to do with that cat we found in the fireplace?"

"I'd forgotten about that. How about we go and get that cup of tea and see what we can find out?" So the couple headed back to their own kitchen and twenty-first century technology, carrying the shoes and bottle.

Matt's cup of tea was getting cold as he became more absorbed in his research. He kept relaying random facts to Rosie who was vigorously attacking the washing up. "Hey, listen to this one," Matt announced with triumph. "It says here that people would put cats behind their walls to keep witches out."

"I already know that!"

"Yes, my dear, but did you know that our ancestors would hide other things in the walls to keep the witches out? In fact, it looks like this bottle is a 'Witch Bottle'. It was meant to trap all the evil and negative energy that the witch wanted to send to the victim. In other words, the witch's spells would get trapped in this bottle and her intended victim would be okay. Apparently, inside this bottle there should be bits of the victim's nail clippings, hair and even some of their urine, as well as some nice, sharp nails and maybe glass. Do you want a look?"

Rosie flinched away from the bottle her husband was thrusting at her. He attempted to remove the cork but it was wedged solid, and after a minute's fruitless efforts he put the bottle aside. Rosie looked at the revolting thing in disgust, praying to the god of accidents that it did not get knocked over. Matt merely returned to the computer.

"The shoes are all part of the plan to trap the witch too. They were put in the chimney to fool the witch into thinking that the person was actually there. But shoes in those days," Matt continued reading, "were very expensive. So the people must have been really scared of witches to make them put their most valuable possession up the chimney. It's all a bit creepy, don't you think? The people who lived here must have been absolutely terrified. Mind you, we are in witch territory, aren't we? Old Matthew Hopkins and his mates."

"What are you going to do with those things?" Rosie asked. She went on to say that she had seen an article about a witchcraft exhibition at a museum in Bury St Edmunds.

"I'll take them there later if you like," Matt offered. "I've got to go out and get some plaster."

"When's later?" Rosie insisted.

Matt looked at his wife and was surprised by what he saw. She was the level-headed one, the one who was fazed by nothing, the one who scoffed at superstition. Yet he could see something approaching fear in her body language.

"Shall I take them now?"

Rosie nodded, "Don't forget that poor little thing in the shed." Matt picked up the objects, then walked over to give Rosie a kiss on her head. But she flinched.

"Please just get those things out of my house." Rosie watched her husband go out to the outhouse where the mummified cat was wrapped in a blanket. She hated irrational feelings and the fear wrought by superstition was probably the most irrational of all fears. She had always prided herself on her ability to avoid such weaknesses. Yet, here she was, scared of witches that did not even exist any more, had probably never existed.

12

"Right, scholars," introduced Mr Carter. "What can you tell our newcomer, Merryn, about Stowmarket?"

That rather unorthodox start to the lesson brought sniggers and subdued chattering from the class.

"It's a dump!" shouted one student.

"There's nothing to do," said another.

"The shops are rubbish," added a third.

"That's a bit harsh, don't you think?" replied the teacher.

"Okay then. Most of it's a dump."

"And most of the shops are rubbish."

"You are entitled to your opinion, of course, although I do not share it," smiled Mr Carter. "What do you know about the history of Stowmarket?"

That brought a more sensible response with contributions mentioning the museum, the Gun Cotton factory explosion in 1871 that killed twenty-eight people, and the bombing of the church in the Second World War. Having an heir to the English throne stationed at the nearby Army Air Corps base was also mentioned.

"What about further back?" the teacher prompted.

That brought a very typical high school response. A lot of the pupils became intent on studying their desks, while many tried to look like they were delving deep into the recesses of their brains to find an answer. "Anything to do with witchcraft?" guessed Jamie.

"Lucky guess?" grinned Mr Carter. "Yes, it is to do with witchcraft. Are you sitting comfortably? Then I'll begin."

And for thirty minutes, the class were entertained with the story of Matthew Hopkins' witch-hunting activities in Stowmarket.

In 1645, he paid his first visit to the town, which resulted in a number of so-called witches being tried. Although the actual number is vague, it is believed that seven men and women hailing from Stowmarket were found to be witches and tried in the assizes at Bury St Edmunds. On the 27th August 1645 a woman called Mary Fuller from Combs was hanged, and other inhabitants of the town who made the history books for being investigated were named as Elizabeth Hubbard, Richard Foreman and William Keeble, although there is no evidence that they were hanged.

In the spring of 1646, the Witch finder General paid a second visit to Stowmarket following a successful witch-hunt in Aldeburgh.

While it is unclear how many witches he caught, the controversy over Hopkins' fees on that occasion are well documented. He was paid more than £23 for his work, which in those days would have been a year's wages for a well-paid craftsman. Also, he claimed expenses for his bed and food in a local inn. This money had to be met by the residents of the town. Sometimes, the witch-hunters were able to demand a share of the witches' property, but most of these witches owned nothing and perhaps there were not enough successful convictions to cover that bill. On 10th April 1646, the people of Stowmarket were ordered to give three shillings each to cover the fees. If they did not pay, they would be put in front of an assize judge.

No longer was Matthew Hopkins a hero who was ridding their town of the evil of witchcraft, he was the man responsible for causing financial hardship in a town already struggling with the debt caused by the Civil War.

"In conclusion," Mr Carter announced to his spellbound audience, "whose side are you on? Would you rid the world of evil at all costs? Or would you put up with the evil spirits and witches that may actually not be witches at all for the sake of keeping hold of your hard earned wages?"

Setting the students the task of writing a letter of justification from Matthew Hopkins, Mr Carter looked round at his pupils and was satisfied. This was every teacher's dream: seeing students working hard and thoroughly enjoying doing so. There was only one blot on his perfect lesson. Merryn Stearne was sitting at her desk and staring out of the window.

"Is anything wrong, Merryn?" he asked approaching her table. As he looked closer, he could see tears forming in her eyes.

"I'm really sorry, sir, but I can't say that he was right in any way. That man was just evil. We don't let people torture each other now, so why should we condone his torture then? Most of them were innocent old women..." The tears slipped from the corners of her eyes and Mr Carter passed her a tissue.

"If you are finding this subject difficult, then I can arrange for you to switch to a different class."

"No," Merryn replied quickly. "I'm really enjoying this subject. It's just too, too...one-sided. It's all about the witch-hunters. I think we should focus on the witches and how they suffered."

"Perhaps that could be the focus of your project. Find out what you can about the real victims of the Stowmarket hunt, or maybe the fates of those who went to trial in Bury St Edmunds."

"If it's okay with you, sir. I am going to focus on the Hitcham witches," Merryn decided. Excused from the task, she read a book to help her research.

"Are you alright, Merryn?" Jamie asked later as they were sitting together on the bus home.

"I'm not sleeping too well, and I keep getting a bit emotional. It's a bit embarrassing really," she blushed.

"Is there anything I can do?"

Merryn could not lose the blush. Remembering her tears in history made her feel embarrassed; but the redness refused to go because of Jamie. He was as near to perfect as any fifteen-year-old boy could be. Not only was he funny and gorgeous, he was also capable of caring about someone's feelings. 'Pull yourself together!' she told herself. 'He's a mate, not a boyfriend, and that's the way it's going to stay.' But she couldn't help hoping. She turned to face the window instead.

"Seriously, why don't you come over to mine tonight? We can watch a DVD or something? Or we could make a start on that project?" Merryn was too amazed to make any sound. Was he asking her out? Surely not. "Don't worry if you're busy. I thought it might be easier if we do the homework together. Get it done quicker."

So that was it – an invitation from a friend, nothing more. Still, that was better than nothing. "That would be really good. How about we do the project for a bit then watch a DVD? I'll bring the new 'Scary Movie' film. Have you seen it?" The time was set and the teenagers returned to their homes, each feeding the butterflies in their stomachs with anticipation.

With three hours to prepare herself for a date that wasn't a date, Merryn skipped into her kitchen and chattered with her parents. She was so happy that Rosie and Matt made a silent mutual decision not to tell her about their sinister finds in the house next door.

Jamie also went home in a buoyant mood. He had never really bothered with the girlfriend scene before having seen the hassle his mates had to go through on a regular basis. He enjoyed the company of girls as friends and thought that was enough. Until now. There was something about Merryn - something different.

It wasn't just that she was really naturally pretty, without having to resort to excessive amounts of make-up. It wasn't just that her green eyes were stunningly cat-like in the way they twinkled in mischief. It wasn't just that she was the most fit girl in year ten. She was also a really good laugh and she did not take herself seriously in any way. Merryn accepted people for what they were and she did not seem to mind that he was a bit of a boff. Plus his mates liked her.

Rob was the only one who knew how Jamie felt. The DVD invitation had been Rob's idea and it looked like it was a good one. Mind you, Jamie had been a bit worried when Merryn hesitated. He thought that she liked him but she kept sending out such weird signals. That time she flinched when he put his arm around her, the way she would look away quickly every time he looked at her, how she would sit next to one of the others if they were all together. Yet Rob convinced him that it was worth a shot. "Trust me," he had said. And Jamie trusted the word of a loser in the girl department. He prayed that he was not about to make the biggest mistake of his life so far.

As he opened the front door, he realised that he couldn't let her come in to this mess. His brother was in the middle of moving out to get settled before his university course began, so there was a collection of packing boxes and bin bags in every available centimetre of floor space. He spent the next couple of hours trying to organise the chaos, and the final hour making himself look clean, presentable and less nervous.

13

It had taken Merryn the full three hours to get ready. After soaking in the bath – they did not have a shower as the house was too stuck in its time-warp for that – she tried on every single combination of outfits in her sparse wardrobe, before deciding on cropped jeans and her favourite blue tee-shirt. Then she put on a hint of make-up and straightened her shoulder-length dark hair.

She felt almost satisfied when she looked in the mirror but still wished she could feel happy with her appearance. Then with an impulsive squirt of her favourite perfume, she went downstairs.

"You look lovely, Merryn. Are you going out?" asked Matt.

"I'm just popping over to Jamie's to watch a DVD," she answered as casually as possible. "I look okay, don't I? I don't look too fat, do I?"

"You are fabulous – my little girl's all grown up," Matt said, pretending to wipe a tear from his eye.

"You look fine. Ignore your dad," smiled Rosie. "He just remembers his little girl in bunches and dungarees. Dads can't cope with their daughters growing up."

"Mum! I am only going to Jamie's to watch a DVD. It's not a date. We are not going out with each other. He's a friend, nothing more. See you later. And, by the way, I hated those dungarees!"

Five minutes later, Merryn was staring, open-mouthed at Jamie. "What do you mean, you have never seen a 'Scary Movie' movie? I know that you have spent your whole life living out here in the sticks but you have the Internet, you've gone digital, you have Blockbuster a few miles away. Therefore you have no excuse."

Jamie punched Merryn playfully on the arm. "Less of the pointy-head stuff, thank you. Just because you used to live in a town with trains and buses and modern things like that."

Their evening was full of laughter and fun. The new movie was better than any of its predecessors, and Jamie and Merryn had felt comfortable in each other's company. There had been no awkward moments, but there had also been no romance. They were too busy watching the movie, chatting and giggling to do anything else.

At nine thirty, Merryn decided that she needed to head home as she had forgotten about a piece of Maths homework. Plus she did not want her parents phoning her to tell her to come home.

"I'll walk you to your door," said Jamie putting on his trainers.

"Don't be so soft," Merryn laughed, "it's hardly a long way."

"Let me be a gentleman. It may be the one and only time in my life I'll ever be chivalrous," was Jamie's exaggeratedly cheesy reaction as he held the door open for her.

It had turned quite windy while they were inside, and now the trees were swaying furiously. It was unusually dark for a May evening, and the leaves brushing back and forward past the houses' outside lights cast elongated, pointy shadows on the paths. Just to complete the effect, the moon was hidden behind a dark cloud.

"Bit spooky," commented Jamie as they walked to Merryn's front door. She did not answer. She was desperate to focus on the path and not The Assembly Room that stood directly to their left hand side. Soon they were at her door, and Merryn could focus her nerves on the impending goodbye.

"Thanks, Jamie, it was great fun tonight. I'm glad I have educated you in the art of decent movies."

"No, I must thank you, Merryn. My life is now complete! And to prove how grateful I am to you for introducing me to the art of the 'Scary Movie', I suggest that we watch another one of them sometime."

Merryn giggled and felt the butterflies attacking her innards again. Would he ask her out? Would he kiss her?

As they got to Merryn's door, Jamie bowed down in an exaggeratedly chivalrous way, then leaned down to open the handle. Merryn was about to slap him on the arm when Snowdrop darted through the gap in the door. They watched helplessly as she sped to the front entrance of The Assembly Room. Without thinking, the teenagers chased after the cat towards the building.

"It's all right. She can't get in," Jamie said. "Those doors are shut tight."

"Are you sure?" Merryn's voice had dropped to a hollow whisper.

They stared at the doors, unable to believe what they were seeing. The round handle on the right hand side of the double doors twisted slowly and the door crept open. As soon as the gap was wide enough, Snowdrop eased her way through. Then the door slammed shut behind her.

Jamie tried to twist the door handle open, but it would not budge. He shoved the door with his shoulder but it was wedged tight. It was as though there was someone or something on the other side, pushing it shut. He looked helplessly at Merryn who was looking terrified.

"She'll be okay in there, Merryn," he said, his chivalry well and truly failed. "She'll probably find a hole in the wall to get out of."

"No, she won't. You don't understand," she sobbed as she ran to her house. Jamie watched her go and knew that he had just blown any chance he had possessed of going out with her. And all because of a stupid cat.

14

The watcher was back in the same building. The difference this time, however, was that she knew where she was: The Assembly Room. It felt like this was the second instalment of a drama series because everything was exactly as it had been at the end of her last dream. The old woman was still tied in the chair, crying from the pain of the wound under her arm. The witch-finder's team stood around her, shooting looks of concern at each other. The same three villagers were watching the proceedings. One of these men was holding up a screwdriver-sized implement and waving it in the face of the witch finder.

"I repeat, Mr Stearne. That woman is no witch. This is all the proof you need. This bodkin drew blood and pain from her so-called 'Devil's Spot'."

"Master Stirman," the witch-finder announced with smarmy pride, his face still indistinguishable under the hat and fancy beard. "I think you will find that you are wrong and I am indeed correct. Look! There is all the proof that you need. As soon as Goodwife Wright cried in pain, her imp came to comfort her!"

The watcher turned to see a small, white cat squeeze through the gap in the door to The Assembly Room. The animal ran to the chair of imprisonment and meowed loudly. She began pacing and rubbing against her mistress's legs. Being unable to get Alice Wright's attention, she cried even louder.

"You see; the imp is talking to her mistress," stated John Stearne. *The witch hunter's assistants nodded and murmured enthusiastically in agreement. They knew that they were in danger of losing this witch because of the failed pricking. To retain their credibility as well as their wages, they needed to nail this one. The presence of the cynical gentlemen watching their every move was certainly not helping.*

"That cat is hungry – nothing more," Master Stirman argued. "Now let Goody Wright go. She is no more a witch than you or I."

That was all that Mr Stearne needed. "You speak of witchcraft as if you have personal knowledge. My intention, and indeed my conscience, is clear. I am doing the work of God. But you, sir, what are you doing? Are you trying to stop me doing God's will? Or are you watching me as you wish to confess? Mr Parsley," he continued turning to his clerk, "Would you be so kind as to talk to the folk outside and ask if there has been any unusual happenings that concern this gentleman here?"

Master Stirman looked at his companions for support but they refused to meet his eyes. How could he have been stupid enough to walk into this trap? He knew that he had few friends in the town. Many of his neighbours were upset at him because he refused to go and fight the troubles with the other men folk. He told them again and again that he was not able to fight because of his weak back but they accused him of cowardice. Raising the rents of those living on his land had not made him popular either. Again, that was not his fault; the troubles had caused him serious problems in his own income. The villagers would love to get their revenge on him, and here there were, being handed the perfect chance to do so.

"Do not be so hasty, sir," he said. "I may have been hasty in my belief in this woman's innocence. Perhaps the bodkin I am holding is defective in some manner. You are the expert in these matters and I bow to your experience and knowledge."

"So you are content to allow us to carry on with our investigation?" John Stearne smirked.

"Yes, sir. I know that you are doing the work of the Lord and, if it is acceptable, I will leave you to continue with your work."

The witch hunter allowed Master Stirman and his companions to reach the door of The Assembly Room before calling to them. "Thank you very much, good sirs, for your help in our investigation today. I do hope you have found that it was fair. I do also hope you support us with our continued questioning of this suspect. I feel content that you did not wish to impede my proceedings and I am sure that your townsfolk will feel the same when you explain it to them."

Master Stirman could feel the threat behind the words and knew it was time to save himself. "Can I do anything to help your investigation?" he asked.

The watcher wanted to yell at the gentleman for his cowardice but no noise would come from her mouth. Master Stirman was going to give them a name, accuse an innocent person just so that he could protect himself. Why did he not just refuse to help the witch hunter do the devil's work? Why did his companions ignore the trickery that was being done? As he opened his mouth, she tried to run to him and make him stop. But she could not move. She was frozen to the spot.

"You are truly a God-fearing man who wishes to do His work, are you? Very well, then. Tell me of other witches in this town and I will see that your conscience is clear." Sometimes, John Stearne felt very smug about how easily he managed to win people over.

Master Stirman took a deep breath and said, "I know of only one: Anne Cricke, who is this woman's neighbour. I have heard a tale that she went to Farmer Waspe to ask for some eggs but he denied her because she had no money to pay him. Then she bewitched his pig. The beast kept shaking his ears, and rubbing them on the trees." He was warming to his story now, becoming as one with the gossips he so often criticised. "The pig was so bewitched that his skin went bald and started bleeding. Farmer Waspe had to cut his ears off. He burnt the ears to try and break the spell. As soon as they finished burning, Goodwife Cricke went to see him to confess what she had done. Anne Cricke is the witch you are seeking, Mr Stearne."

As the liar spoke his poison, the watcher saw a myriad of emotions cover Alice Wright's face. Shock was the initial reaction, followed by anger and sorrow. Then a gloomy resignation settled there – it seemed as though the old woman knew that someone else was being lined up to suffer in the same way that she had.

"Thank you very much," replied the witch hunter. "You have been very helpful indeed and I look forward to seeing you soon. Maybe you will be able to help me again." He held the door open for the farmer and his shame faced companions, then listened to the crowd beyond braying for news of the witch inside. As the door shut, he heard the man tell his enraptured audience all about the spot that did not bleed and about the woman's admission that she consorted with the devil as a child.

Mr Stearne smiled and shut the door. The smile became a frown as he looked at Alice Wright. "Now, Goodwife Wright, we have a problem. You have failed my tests so far but before justice can be served at the assizes, I need you to confess. Tell me why you consorted with the devil when you were a child. Tell me why you continue to practise his work."

Alice looked at him with pure hatred in her eyes. She had no pride left, sitting in this wooden chair covered only with an itchy, woollen blanket that Goody Mills had placed over her. There was so much pain coming from the mark under her arm but she did not want to show her discomfort. Instead of answering, she glared even more.

The white cat could obviously sense the atmosphere and was becoming increasingly upset. She was pacing backwards and forwards, a low growl coming from her throat. Suddenly, the witch hunter reached down and grabbed the cat by the scruff of her neck. His arm was outstretched and he dangled the yowling feline in front of Alice's face. Although his words were aimed at someone else, he spoke them to his victim. "Take the imp out of here and throw it in the pond!"

Goody Mills hurried to collect the cat that was now hissing and flailing helplessly. But as she took hold of it, she caught Alice's eye and tried to send an unspoken message that her pet would be all right. She would put the pet outside, as ordered, but it would be nowhere near the pond.

The watcher's vision began to blur with tears, as Alice watched her only friend being taken from her. Now the old woman was truly alone.

Merryn woke with a start, the images of the nightmare flickering and fading in her head, her pillow damp with tears. She looked in the darkness of her room and tried to listen for strange noises. But there was nothing except blackness and silence. She decided that she must have been woken by the dream, so she wriggled back down under her duvet. Merryn tried to stretch her legs out but she couldn't. There was something in the way. Reaching down she felt the soft fur of Snowdrop. The pet she last saw disappearing into The Assembly Room was back as if nothing had ever happened. Furthermore, she was purring with utter contentment.

15

Merryn spent the weekend keeping as busy as possible. It gave her less time to think. And she had too much to dwell on.

On Friday morning, she sat with Jamie on the bus as usual, but he had not been his normal self. He spent more time turning round to talk to the people behind him than speaking to her. He asked after Snowdrop and said that he was pleased she was back, but he asked for no more details. Merryn longed to tell him about her dream, but he was too remote for that.

Merryn came to the conclusion that he obviously did not fancy her. Yesterday evening had shown him that she was a friend – nothing more. She must have blown it by being such a coward and running away from The Assembly Room. Subconsciously, she was scowling as those thoughts caused havoc in her tormented mind. She shuffled her body round as she turned to gaze out of the window so that her back was facing Jamie.

In fact, Jamie was kicking himself that he hadn't made more of an effort last night. He really wanted to tell Merryn that he had feelings for her, but he chickened out. He was about to say something when her annoying cat ran away. After that, he had looked like a total idiot when he could not even open The Assembly Room door to rescue the cat. It was clear that she thought he was a loser. She had hardly said two words to him today, and all she could do now was glare into space. It was quite obvious that she did not want to be sitting with him. She had even turned her back on him.

It was not just Jamie that was concerning Merryn; she was also getting very worried about her dreams. She knew that they must have come from the amount of research she had been doing for her history project. But she was dreaming things that she had not read about. Plus they felt too real - like she was actually there, like she was a part of the events. She was even starting to be afraid of going to sleep at night.

She wanted to talk to someone about it. But who? Her parents knew that she was having nightmares but she could not tell them why. They had too much to worry about what with the renovation work and the job hunting. Also, they would want to help and that would involve seeking logical answers and maybe medical interventions. Merryn knew that, despite her own previously cynical beliefs, her dreams could not be explained away by science alone. Maria and Lily would just think she was a total freak if she bared her soul, and Jamie was hardly talkative. At that moment in time, Merryn felt as alone as the old woman in her dreams.

To take her mind off her troubles, she volunteered to help her dad in the neighbouring house the next day - Saturday. Their task was to demolish the wall between the kitchen and the pantry to create a larger space, then put an archway between the spaces. The supports were in place to keep the ceiling intact and Matt had an enormous piece of steel waiting outside to make the new lintel.

She had been very disappointed when she was told that they could not use a sledgehammer as Merryn hoped to take some of her stress out on the wall. But Matt wanted to do things the right way, and knock the bricks through carefully to minimise damage.

Two hours later, with the bricks paying testament to the skills of house builders in the medieval times, Matt handed Merryn the sledgehammer. "Told you it would be easier," she commented after a few successful smashes.

"I was just worried about whacking any more dodgy stuff," replied Matt. As soon as he spoke the words, he remembered that he and Rosie had vowed not to tell their daughter about their grisly find.

"What are you on about?" asked Merryn.

"Nothing important," Matt muttered. "Pass me that sledgehammer and I'll pretend it's my old boss."

Merryn held tight to the tool. "Not until you tell me what you are talking about."

Not wishing to argue with a hormonal teenager wielding a weapon of destruction, Matt told Merryn about the shoes and the witch's bottle he had discovered in the walls of the house.

"They're meant to keep witches away," Merryn said. "People thought that if they put something of their own into the walls of a house, then it would catch all the evil spirits and protect them from witches and stuff. Bricking up live cats was meant to scare off other witch's familiars."

"You know a lot about it," was all Matt could say. He felt a bit disturbed by his daughter's reaction. He had expected her to be shocked, maybe a bit disgusted – not calm and analytical, as though she was reciting from a textbook.

Merryn told her father about the project at school and relayed everything that she knew about the Suffolk witch-hunts. When she paused, he was lost for words again. "They must have been really superstitious here. It seems a bit weird though that there are counter spells in houses where witches were meant to live," she commented.

That comment made Matt regain his sense of speech. "What do you mean? How do you know witches lived here? There's no record of anything like that in the deeds."

"Well, there wouldn't be, would there? In those days, no one was proud of having witches in their community. That's why it's so hard to find evidence. What is it we call it now? Political spin? They wrote down what they wanted people to know and that wasn't always the truth. Just like today."

"But that doesn't answer my question," Matt persisted. "How do you know - if there are no records?"

"I just know. Alice Wright lived in our house and Anne Cricke lived in this one. And John Stearne tried them in The Assembly Room. Somewhere in the back garden, there is a large pond. Have you found it yet?"

Matt was getting worried. Merryn seemed to be going into some sort of trance. She was talking in a monotone voice, as though she was delivering the same lecture for the thousandth time. As soon as she finished talking, she calmly laid down the sledgehammer and walked through the back door into the garden.

He watched from a distance as she moved slowly but purposefully around the large, overgrown area. Merryn was obviously looking for something and she kept stamping at the parched ground with her foot.

She continued doing this for a full five minutes until she stopped at the left hand side of the garden. Merryn was standing directly behind The Assembly Room but about thirty metres away. She was in a roughly rectangular area of brambles and long grass, ravaged by time and neglect. A large oak tree stood at one corner and a branch sturdy enough to hold a swing hung over the patch of wilderness.

"I've found it, Dad," Merryn yelled to her bemused father. "I've found the pond. This is where they swum the witch."

16

Matt and Rosie were sitting at the kitchen table, their cups of tea going cold as they watched Merryn in the distance, frantically weeding the patch of garden that she claimed was a pond.

Matt told his wife what had happened and they immediately researched what they could on the Internet. Merryn's allegations turned out to be true – at least some of them were. John Stearne had swept through the village taking at least two witches with him: Alice Wright and Anne Cricke. But as for the idea that the women used to live in these houses and faced trial in The Assembly Room; there was absolutely no evidence of that. That must have been the result of an over-active imagination.

What troubled them more now was Merryn's behaviour. She was always so sensible and, while not excessively lazy, she would choose the easy route if possible. However, she was pulling away at the large patch of weeds like a girl possessed. She was even ripping brambles and nettles from the ground with her bare hands. Matt tried to stop her but she calmly turned her back to him saying, "I'm just trying to find the pond."

On Saturday evening, Merryn uprooted and pulled her final weed. Then she walked into the kitchen covered in dirt from the dry soil, her nails broken to the quick and her clothing ripped by the brambles. "I'll just get a quick bath then get some tea. Is that okay?" With that she skipped out of the room.

"Did we imagine that?" Matt asked Rosie.

"Which bit? The normal daughter or the psychotic gardener?"

Rosie found it easier than her husband to find one hundred and one logical reasons for the bizarre behaviour. However, no matter how convincing they sounded, Matt felt very uneasy.

Merryn's parents slept in until ten o'clock the following morning. They assumed that their daughter was still asleep as there was not a squeak from her room. How wrong they were, as they discovered when they went into the kitchen.

Merryn was busy digging in the area in which she had been weeding the previous day. She must have been at it for a while as there were mounds of earth everywhere. She saw them watching and waved at them, an enormous grin covering her face. Matt and Rosie grabbed a cup of tea then hurried upstairs to put on scruffy clothes. If Merryn was determined to create a pond, they would just have to help her.

Thirty minutes later, the Stearne family were digging through solid earth. The weather, which had been repeatedly called 'glorious' by the forecasters, was proving a hindrance to them. They may have been developing a 'glorious' suntan, but their spades were not as happy. "Can't we do this later?" moaned Matt.

"There's a pond down here somewhere," Merryn answered not looking up from her work. "You don't have to help if you don't want to. It's not your responsibility."

Rosie glared at Matt as a warning not to argue with his daughter. So he headed into the house to fetch some water. He returned fifteen minutes later with something more.

Jamie and his father, Nick, were walking across the garden carrying spades. Merryn's heart skipped as she watched them approach but she felt extremely nervous at the same time. "I found these two on the front door. They said something about a barbecue at their house tonight. But I had to negotiate a bit of muscle power before I accepted. They didn't seem to complain too much."

Merryn cringed at her dad's embarrassing behaviour and glanced at Jamie. He was giving her a sympathetic look that said, "I know all about annoying parents." She felt a warm glow that even the sun could not beat, and all her anxiety from Friday melted away. They headed to the far end of the digging patch and left the parents to discuss boring parent issues.

"You must be losing it, Merryn," said Jamie earning himself a slap on the arm. "It's boiling hot, there are so many more interesting things you could be doing on a Sunday afternoon, and here you are digging a massive hole in your garden just because you want a pond. Can't we just fill a bucket with a bit of water?"

"I'm not going mad, honestly," she replied. "I just had an urge to dig down here and find a pond. Don't ask me why. Maybe I've got sunstroke or something."

"It's the something I'm worried about!" Instead of the slapped arm he had been expecting, Jamie received a squirt from Merryn's water bottle. He had no choice but to try and wrestle it from her.

The three adults were watching the teenagers' water-fight while Rosie described Merryn's strange behaviour to Nick. He could not offer any explanation but expressed a lot of sympathy. How he had been able to help was with a geological lesson on the area.

Nick told them that there could well have been a pond on that site. There was a natural hedgerow running alongside the area that continued across the fields beyond to a wood. "There's a lake in those woods," he explained, "and a stream runs from it towards us. But the stream goes underground about half way across the field behind us. There's no sign of it beyond The Assembly Room so it is entirely feasible that it ends up here."

With renewed determination, the adults went to help their children dig. It was not in vain. After nearly three hours and one metre of digging, Merryn yelled. "I've hit water!"

There was not a lot of it. It was not even a trickle, merely a drip. But there was definitely water. It took a further two hours for the workers, now joined by Jamie's mother, Jane, to level the rest of the patch. Forgetting the ludicrousness of the situation, they all celebrated as they uncovered the underground spring that would eventually feed this pond. Once the rain returned, that is.

The subsequent barbecue was jovial and highly successful. The parents shared their life stories and conjectured about the true nature of their children's feelings for each other, leaving Jamie and Merryn to chat awkwardly.

"Is your cat alright now?" asked Jamie.

"Yeah," said Merryn. "She's fine. Just came back like nothing had happened."

"How's your history project going?" Jamie wanted to ask something different but he could not find the right words. Besides, he couldn't ask Merryn out with his parents standing there. That would just have been so wrong. Instead, they talked about trivia – that was safer.

Spending an evening of food and fun in the Fosters' garden meant that no one saw the pond slowly filling with water from a parched stream-bed.

17

The watcher was standing around the edge of the pond that lay behind The Assembly Room. She recognised it as the pond she had uncovered that very afternoon. There were a lot of other people there, mostly women, although she could see the farmer, Master Stirman with his fellow war shirkers. They were all waiting in anticipation, chattering and laughing. It was a strange atmosphere. It was as though they were waiting for a show, for the arrival of a celebrity.

Suddenly a hush fell over the crowd and everyone turned to face The Assembly Room. Alice Wright was being led around the side of the building towards her waiting audience, her head bent low. Holding her arms at either side were two women who the watcher recognised as Goody Phillips and Goody Mills. On several occasions, the woman stumbled and was caught by Goody Mills. The other woman simply tutted and pushed the prisoner harshly in the ribs to make her stand upright.

Walking behind the women were four men. Two of them she recognised as sons of the farmer. They were tall, strong men accustomed to heavy tasks; one was carrying a thick, long rope, the other a large pole. Following them were two better-dressed men: one was holding what appeared to be official documents and a leather case, and the other walked with an arrogant swagger, clearly in command of the whole situation and thoroughly enjoying his position.

The farmer's sons shouted to some of the onlookers to clear an area at the narrower edge of the pond. With the rubberneckers displaced, the old woman was told to lie on the ground in a foetal position. She did not resist at all, and remained passive as her left toe was tied to her right thumb and her right toe was tied to her left thumb.

Alice Wright kept her eyes fully averted, ignoring the jeers of the crowd. Once she was trussed up, the large rope was tied around her waist. Pushing the crowd away from the edge of the pond, the farmer's sons each took an end of the rope and started to walk to either side of the long edges of the pond. When they were half way down, they stopped and looked at the man in charge.

John Stearne took his time in addressing the audience, first looking around at all the expectant faces and waiting for the moment of most impact.

"Ladies and gentlemen, I am here to carry out the work of God. This woman has failed two trials of witchcraft, and has confessed to consorting with the devil as a child. However," he shouted over the sudden rise in noise level, "I am a fair man and I wish to see justice done. So I will conduct one further trial to test whether Goody Wright is a witch.

"We will try her by 'swimming'. She will be lowered into this pond three times. If Goody Wright sinks, and remains, under the water, then she will be deemed innocent and will be set free. If she floats, that is proof of her guilt and she will be sent to the assizes to be tried in court as a witch." The crowd cheered in response, screaming for justice and shouting 'float, float, float'.

Even that final flourish brought no reaction from the forlorn old woman. It was as though she had already accepted her fate and just wanted it to be over. Alice Wright was so thin and small that it took only the strength of Edward Parsley to lift her into the water's edge. She was placed on her back with her limbs curled upwards, and the farmer's sons tightened the rope dragging her towards the centre of the pond. Although her back was becoming submersed, she appeared to be floating.

"Try again," ordered the witch hunter. The ropes were pulled tighter and Alice rose above the water for a brief moment. This time she showed emotion. She was staring upwards and seemed to be speaking. Then they lowered her into the water and the tension loosened in the rope. Her body twisted so that she was on her side and she started to sink. As Alice went down, the watcher caught her eye.

It seemed like she was staring at Alice for a lifetime, but it cannot have been more than seconds. She saw absolute terror in her eyes, and a look of beseeching. Her eyes pleaded with the watcher to help her, but her lips were moving in prayer. The watcher heard no words pass her lips, but she knew that Alice was speaking 'The Lord's Prayer'. The watcher tried to shout. "She is innocent! She is innocent!" However, no words could pass her lips. She wanted to jump into the pond and pull Alice out but she was unable to move. Alice locked eyes with the watcher as she sank below the surface.

"She may yet be innocent, ladies and gentlemen," John Stearne declared. "For the third time, bring her up and we will give her another chance." Alice Wright was pulled up from the water, gasping and choking, but not struggling.

For the third and final time, the watcher saw the barbaric act of this helpless wretch being dropped below the surface. As with the first time, she stayed on her back with her arms and legs upright. By now, the bloodthirsty crowd were making frenzied cries yelling for the death of the witch.

Suddenly, John Stearne stepped forward with the pole that had been left at the side of the pond. He poked Alice in the side so that she spun over, face down into the water.

The watcher caught her eye just before Alice Wright made her final descent. "I'm sorry," the watcher mouthed, tears streaming down her face. The old woman merely smiled in return, the terror in her eyes replaced by a serene calmness. It was as though she had finally found peace.

This time as Alice went below the water, the witch hunter pushed the pole firmly into her side so that she could not come back up. For a full five minutes, an absolute silence fell as the rabble waited for an outcome to the trial. Then the pole was pulled away, the ropes were tightened and the body of Alice Wright slowly rose to the surface.

Some screamed, some merely drew sharp intakes of breath, some made the signs of the cross and some said a prayer asking forgiveness for their evil thoughts. Only a few thought of the poor wretch who had been sacrificed for their entertainment and narrow-minded opinions. Then they thanked themselves that justice had been served and carried on with their own lives.

The watcher stayed still – she could not do anymore – and watched as Alice's body was wrapped in a thick blanket. She heard the priest give directions to the farmer's sons. That cowardly man had watched the whole performance from a safe distance away from his parishioners and had not seen fit to intervene. They were to take the body to the churchyard and instruct the gravedigger to dig a hole in the pauper's graveyard.

Alice Wright had died with no family and no money. All she possessed was her house, but that was already promised to John Stearne as payment for his services. As her body was carried away and everyone had gone, the watcher saw a small, white cat pad across to the side of the pond. It sniffed at the water and meowed softly, then sadly trailed away into the fields beyond.

Rosie had been woken up by strange noises coming from Merryn's room. She was horrified by what she saw when she entered. Merryn was lying on her side, curled on top of her bed with her toes and fingers touching. She was gasping for breath and turning a dreadful shade of blue. Rosie grabbed hold of her daughter to pull her upright, thinking that she was choking.

She felt a freezing cold wetness coming from her daughter's body. Instantly, she discounted it as sweat or urine as it was too wide covering, and it had more of an earthy smell. Rosie could hardly believe it. Merryn was soaked through, as though she had been submerged under water.

Suddenly the gasping stopped and Merryn relaxed. She sank into her mother's arms and smiled, then flopped into an apparent state of lifelessness. Terrified, Rosie felt for a pulse. She found one almost immediately, and it was a slow, strong pulse – something you would expect from someone in a deep sleep.

Rosie laid her daughter back down on the bed and went to fetch a towel. She placed it over the sleeping child expecting it to get wet straight away, but it did not. In the minute that it had taken to leave the room and find a towel, Merryn had gone from being soaked through to merely a little damp.

She longed to wake her child, to demand an answer to what had just happened. However, Merryn looked so serene just lying there that Rosie did not dare to wake her. Instead she went back to bed, but could not sleep again. Images of Merryn apparently drowning in her bed filled her troubled head and sleep was not allowed a look in.

18

"Where were you this morning, skiver?" Jamie asked when Merryn strolled into afternoon registration.

"Mum took me to the doctor's. She reckoned I was having something like an asthma attack last night because I couldn't breathe."

"Are you okay?"

"Yeah, I'm fine," Merryn said. "The doctor reckons I just got a bit of heatstroke from yesterday."

"It was a bit manic digging that pond," he grinned.

Merryn smiled back at him, blushing a bit as she remembered how much of a laugh they'd had. "Fun though!"

Rob was sitting with Lily, Maria and Ed. For the past few weeks they had been running bets on how long it would take for Jamie and Merryn to get together. Being typically skint teenagers, the prize was a chocolate bar from each of the losers.

Ed and Marcus had lost interest when their guess of 'within a couple of weeks of their first meeting' had come and gone. They were also a little bemused as to why it was taking so long. Lily and Maria kept saying 'any day now', but had been forced to delay their prediction to sometime in 'June'. Rob had been reluctant to join in, knowing how useless Jamie was with girls. He would probably never find the courage to do anything about his feelings. But he agreed to set a tentative date of 'by the end of term'. Watching them now, Rob thought he would probably owe both Lily and Maria a chocolate bar.

On the bus home, Jamie turned to Merryn and became serious. "You know, I was worried about you at the weekend."

"Why?"

"Well, not me, really – more like my parents. Not that I wasn't worried but I didn't think it was a big deal. Maybe I should just shut up."

"No way," Merryn said. "You don't get away with it that easily. Why is everyone worried about me all of a sudden?"

Jamie breathed a sigh of relief as the bus pulled up outside their houses. He was about to well and truly blow it if he was not careful. But Merryn was not giving up.

"I want to know what you are going on about!" She looked at him closely and saw that he was looking really awkward and embarrassed, and Merryn started feeling sorry for him. "Do you fancy coming over to mine for a while? Then you can confess! Mum and Dad are out till later on – it's their wedding anniversary and they've gone shopping in Norwich. So no-one will hear your screams if you don't confess."

Another sigh of relief was breathed and Jamie followed Merryn obediently.

A short while later, they were sitting at the kitchen table. Jamie had suggested that they sit in the garden, but Merryn refused. After her dream last night, she could not face looking at the pond. "But you spent hours on it all weekend," Jamie declared, totally perplexed.

"So you are all worried about me are you? Well, if I tell you something, will you promise not to think I'm a total lunatic until I've finished?" Merryn knew that she was taking a huge risk, but she had to talk. With all the dreams, and all the other weird happenings – Snowdrop's behaviour, the bleeding, the sudden uncontrollable urge to build a pond, the way that she knew things that she could not possibly know – she needed to off-load.

"I've been having these dreams..." She told Jamie the whole story and he did not interrupt once. Occasionally he would add a 'go on' or 'I'm listening', but otherwise he was fully engaged in her story.

Twenty minutes later, they sat together in stunned silence. Jamie did not know what to say. He had known that Merryn was terrified of The Assembly Room, and that the whole witch heritage freaked her out. When her cat disappeared that night, he thought it was just annoying, nothing more. Now, he was not so sure.

"You don't believe me, do you?" Merryn muttered.

"It's not that I don't believe you," he replied. "It's that I don't understand. It's like you were actually there, watching all the witch hunt trials, but how can you have been?"

"And if I was just watching, how come I got some of the symptoms like the bleeding and the nearly dying?"

"You are asking for logical answers, but there is nothing logical about any of this. That is not to say it's not happening. But there's more. It's like there's more to it than just you. What about your cat? What happened to her is nothing to do with you. And digging the pond? You did that before you had the dream. I'm sorry, Merryn. I can't get my head round this. I'm a boy – I don't do superstition."

"Neither did I," sulked Merryn before she fell silent. She knew that Jamie did not believe her but at least she couldn't be accused of lying to him or hiding things from him. Therefore, she was totally shocked by his next remarks.

"You know, my mum has always said that The Assembly Room is haunted. Once, when she was walking the dog past that place, she reckoned she saw the face of an old woman at the window, even though you can't see through the windows."

"I saw that!" Merryn interrupted excitedly. "I've seen her twice! It's Alice Wright – the one who they drowned in the pond. I forgot to tell you about that bit."

"Do you think so? My mum also reckons she has heard noises from there too, like people shouting and a woman screaming," he continued. "She won't go anywhere near the place now. My dad had to literally drag her over to help you dig your pond. So, yes, I do believe you, I think - I just don't get it."

"Do you reckon it will stop now Alice Wright has died in my dreams?"

Jamie was reluctant to answer. He did not want to be dragged into such an irrational discussion; then again, he wanted to show Merryn that he supported her. So he took the stance of combining belief with reason. "I'm not sure. She wasn't the only Hitcham witch, as you know. It depends on who's actually haunting you. If Alice is haunting you, then it should stop. But if it's something other than Alice, then I'm not so sure. Whatever happens, Merryn, I'll be around to help you get through it. Okay?"

Merryn could not answer; she was too ecstatic. Jamie believed her and he said he would be there for her. He must care. At that moment, Matt and Rosie returned with take-away pizza – enough for all four of them – and Jamie was saved from having to worry about whether the girl he was falling in love with was slightly insane.

19

The half term holidays passed in a rather boring way. Jamie and his family went away to Italy for the week, leaving Merryn in charge of Cadbury - the Fosters' chocolate Labrador. She was so attentive to her charge that she did not have the time to worry about witches and haunted buildings.

One evening, following another session by Merryn attempting to make her parents agree to get a dog, Matt announced his surprise plan. "Someone has her fifteenth birthday coming up in a few weeks - 20th of June, I believe - and that someone may want to have a bit of a party for all her friends."

"Oh, wow. Are you serious? Thanks, Dad!" Merryn jumped up and hugged him.

"Just wait a minute. You might not like what I am suggesting."

"So long as it doesn't involve inviting revolting cousin Ruby, I will like it," countered Merryn.

"She is top of the guest list," Matt joked. "How do you fancy a marquee in the garden, with a barbecue and a disco? I've already spoken to the neighbours about it and they are fine so long as they get a beer and a burger. Though I'm sure one neighbour will be getting a personal invitation!"

Merryn slapped her father on the arm, then hugged him again. "Thank you so much. It's going to be fantastic." The conversation then steered towards the number of guests, timing and other fine details. Within half an hour, Merryn was chatting to Lily and Maria on the Internet, discussing outfits and a possible guest list.

"Hopefully that will stop her going on about the dog," commented Rosie. "I don't want that surprise spoilt. What are we going to do if the weather changes?"

"It's not meant to," Matt replied. "They reckon this heat wave will last right through until the end of July, then there'll be torrential rain for the summer holidays, as usual. I am optimistic that we will be absolutely fine for the big day."

As anyone that has ever relied on a father's optimism knows, it is not reliable.

Merryn spent three weeks getting herself organised for her party. She went shopping to both Ipswich and Bury St Edmunds to hunt for the perfect dress, only to find one in a small independent shop in Stowmarket. The friendships she had been building with Lily and Maria were now set in concrete, and she spent a lot of time with Jamie discussing play lists for the DJ as well as sorting out refreshments.

The party was due to take place on the Saturday, which was the day of Merryn's actual birthday. On Friday, everyone had gone to school in baking hot sunshine but by ten thirty, a black cloud descended over Hitcham and the surrounding areas. It stayed there for the entire day, threatening rain without delivering.

"I don't like the look of that cloud," Matt muttered to Rosie when he came from their neighbouring house to get a cup of tea.

"It's a bit odd," she agreed. "There's no sign of it at all on the national weather forecast, but on the local one, it calls it 'totally unexpected'. I wish it would either shed its load and move on, or just disappear as quickly as it came. I am a bit worried though. If it rains tomorrow, they can't have a party in a marquee."

"I've already thought of that. As soon as I finish this, I'm going to The Assembly Room and give it a good tidy up. She can have the party in there."

"But she hates that place!"

"She'll hate missing her party even more," Matt reasoned. "Besides, once it's cleaned and decorated, it will look okay. Do you fancy leaving your studying and giving me a hand?"

So Merryn's parents headed for The Assembly Room clutching brooms, dusters and a large supply of bin bags.

Rosie had not been in there before. As soon as she walked through the thick wooden door, she felt the temperature plummet. She told herself that it must be something to do with the damp and lack of use. But she did not know how to explain away the hairs prickling on the back of her neck, or the feeling she had that she was an unwelcome visitor.

She did not tell Matt how she was feeling for fear of seeming ridiculous. She was a grown woman studying for one of the most logical, analytical jobs ever – accountancy – and she was being frightened by an old, scruffy collection of bricks and crumbling mortar. If Rosie had shared her feelings, however, she may have been surprised to find that he was experiencing exactly the same.

"It's impossible to do anything in here when it's as dark as this," said Matt. "I'm going to go and get some glass for those window frames. Do you want to come?" Matt did not want to leave Rosie in this place alone. He did not know why, and he would never tell her for fear of being condescending. But he just knew that leaving her alone in this miserable place was a potential disaster.

They measured the frames and left, both relieved to be breathing in the stuffy, humid air of the countryside.

By the time the school bus pulled up, Matt had replaced the windows at the hedge side of the building where Merryn would not notice the changes. Rosie was waiting in the kitchen for her daughter, bracing herself for an enormous sulk.

"Mum, look at that cloud. It is going to chuck it down tomorrow. I'm going to have to cancel. We can't have an outside party in the pouring rain," Merryn wailed.

"Don't worry. We have thought of that," reassured Rosie. "If it is really awful tomorrow, we'll take you all out for pizza instead."

"But that will cost a fortune! There are about twenty people coming."

"I know. Just remember how much we will be saving on the DJ, the drinks and all that stuff. It will probably cost about as much."

"But it won't be the same!"

"I know," Rosie said. "But it's called making the most of an unfortunate situation. Anyway, who knows? This may have passed over by tomorrow."

Merryn could not be consoled and huffed to her bedroom, while Rosie went to join her husband in The Assembly Room. She could already see the improvement; it was a shame she couldn't feel it.

20

Three dramatic events happened on the morning of Merryn's party. The first two were dramatically good; the third could have been dramatically awful.

Merryn's mobile phone beeped to show an incoming text message at eight thirty in the morning. She was just rubbing the sleep from her eyes so she had to read the text twice to make sure she had got it right. It was from Jamie.

"Happy Birthday! I don't want to ruin your day but I need to do this before someone else does. Will you go out with me?"

Merryn spent a minute hugging her pillow to her chest with an enormous cheesy grin stretching the muscles on her face. Then she texted back: "YES!"

Very quickly, she received a message in reply: "I cannot believe you said yes. Will you be about in half an hour? I have a present for you." Merryn replied with another 'yes' and an 'x', then hurried to the bathroom to get ready. She was too excited to notice that the heavy purply black rain cloud was still there and looking even more ominous.

She walked down the creaky stairs to an extra loud "Happy Birthday" being sung by her mum, Jamie and his parents. The pile of presents on the kitchen table was disappointingly small, but Merryn still smiled with gratitude. "Open your others first," directed Rosie. "You can do your main ones when Dad gets back."

Jamie's dad handed her a card, in which she found a £20 i-Tunes voucher. "I've lost touch with modern music," he apologised, "and we thought this would be safer."

Merryn hugged him and Jamie's mum, overwhelmed at their generosity. Then Jamie stepped across to her.

As they looked at each other, they simultaneously blushed and smiled. He was holding two gifts and he handed her a rectangular shaped package. She ripped off the paper and opened the lid of the gift box to reveal a silver bracelet with a variety of charms on it. There was a small dog, a cat, a letter 'M', a witch's hat and a broomstick. She grinned wider than the proverbial Cheshire puss, and hugged a scarlet Jamie.

Then he handed her the second package. It was a weird shape; sort of bumpy and squishy. She tore off the paper and gasped when the gift was revealed. It was a pink, fake diamond studded puppy collar and matching lead.

At that moment, and under command from his wife, Matt walked in carrying a wriggling, chocolate brown bundle with a pink ribbon around its neck. He handed the eight-week-old Labrador to Merryn.

"She's Cadbury's puppy," said Matt. "You enjoyed having him around so much that I had a word with Nick and Jane. Cadbury had just been used for stud, so I got in touch with the bitch's owner and managed to get first choice of the litter. She's got a full pedigree so she can be taken to shows or bred with."

The puppy decided that she was fed up of being cuddled, so Merryn put her down and she began to sniff her new surroundings. Snowdrop chose that moment to walk through the kitchen towards the garden, only to have her way blocked by a playful furry lump. The cat sniffed the new arrival's nose, then sauntered outside as if she finding a puppy in her kitchen was totally uncool and wholly unworthy of her attention.

Then Merryn opened her other presents, mostly accessories for her new companion, clothes, smellies or chocolate. She had also been given a giant 'Galaxy' bar. "I've got a great idea!" she said.

"What? Go on a diet starting from now and give your dad all that chocolate," suggested Matt.

Merryn gave him the look that only teenagers can do well: the withering look meant to reverse the adult/youth role that says, "I will acknowledge your attempt at humour even though you have a lot to learn about jokes."

"No, Dad, but I will share a little bit. I'm going to call her Galaxy."

At first the few drops of rain went unnoticed as everyone was fussing little Galaxy. It was only when Rosie went to the sink to fill the kettle that she saw the drops turning heavier. Matt came to stand next to her and spoke in a whisper. "Plan B is ready. Nick and Jane helped me finish off the final bits this morning and I've already spoken to the DJ. Don't worry. It's all sorted."

Just then, Merryn spotted the rain. "Oh no," she wailed. "Look at the weather. I can't have a party in this. I'll have to cancel."

Matt put his arm around his daughter's shoulder. "I've got something to show you. Jamie, you come too."

Merryn picked up the puppy, then she and Jamie followed Matt. She stopped abruptly when she saw that he was heading for The Assembly Room.

"I am not going in there," she announced.

"It's either that or stay out here and get wet," shouted Matt over the noise of the rain.

Jamie looked at Merryn, shrugged and carried on. She had no choice but to go with them. Matt pushed open the door and stepped back.

Merryn stared in amazement. The place was transformed. There were pink, purple and white balloons all over the floor and window frames, and bunting covered the walls. Some tables were placed at the side of the room draped in pink tablecloths with a small vase of flowers in the middle of each. Chairs had been covered with ribbon, and there was a large table at the end of the room, with glasses arranged in a pyramid at one side, plates and serviettes at the other and a chocolate fountain in the centre. Above the table was an enormous banner reading, "Happy Birthday, Merryn."

With tears in her eyes, Merryn put Galaxy down and hugged her dad. "You need to hug him too," he said, referring to Jamie. "We were doing this late last night." Merryn turned to her boyfriend and squeezed him tight. That hug would have lasted a lot longer except that Galaxy started nipping at their feet.

Back at the house, Merryn realised what was missing in The Assembly Room. She had not felt any hostility in there: no drop in temperature, no whispering voices to get out. It was just any old building with no witches, ghosts or remnants from the past. Even with the horrendous weather, nothing could possibly put a dampener on the day, could it?

21

The party was a terrific success. Everyone who had been invited turned up, the DJ was excellent and refused to play 'YMCA', the decorations were complimented and the food was delicious. The barbecue had been abandoned, so baguette pizzas, Pringles and other nibbles were served. However, it was the chocolate fountain that had been most successful especially with the dunked jelly babies.

At ten thirty, most of the guests left, leaving behind Merryn, Jamie, Rob, Ed, Marcus, Lily and Maria. They had agreed to stay behind and tidy up in return for a sleepover at Merryn's house.

"Wait there," Merryn said when they were alone. "I want you to meet someone." Jamie had been unable to keep the secret from them as well, so it came as no surprise when a boisterous brown lump of fur hurtled through the door and set about jumping all over them.

It took a long time to clear up; mostly because Galaxy was helping rather too enthusiastically. But eventually, the floor was clear, the decorations were down and the tables were stripped. It no longer looked pretty but to Merryn, the room still felt cosy.

The friends were sitting on the floor finishing off the last of the fruit punch when Ed came up with a suggestion. "How do you fancy having the sleepover in here?" Other than Jamie and Merryn, everyone was eager to do this. Marcus saw their trepidation and set to convincing them. It worked and five minutes later, Merryn and Jamie were heading to the house to collect sleeping bags and pillows.

"I'm still not happy about this," said Merryn.

"I know," replied Jamie, "but you can't disappoint the others. Besides, it's been okay in there tonight, hasn't it? You haven't had any bad feelings, have you?"

"No, I haven't. And you are right. I don't want to let them down. Maybe I was just being superstitious."

"There's nothing wrong with being superstitious," countered Jamie. "Maybe it's all over now. Maybe it all finished with Alice's death. How about this? We'll stay in there but we can go if you are feeling weird at all."

Merryn hugged Jamie in reply, then held his hand as they carried on walking.

"Wondered where you two love birds had gone," Lily teased on their return.

"How did you know?" Merryn spluttered.

Rob smiled. "Come on, it was pretty obvious you two would get together. Right, who's up for ghost stories before bed time?"

As Merryn and Jamie shouted 'no' simultaneously, Ed stood up. "I'm going to find a bush outside, seeing as this place don't have no toilets. Don't start without me!" He walked across to the door and pulled it, but it would not move.

"Very funny. Which one of you two locked the door?"

"It's not locked," Merryn replied with terror nudging at her voice. "There is no lock." So Ed pulled harder, but it still would not move. Rob, Marcus, Lily and Maria went to help him but their efforts were also fruitless.

"I'll phone my dad," Merryn whispered. She was starting to feel very cold as though the temperature had dropped by ten degrees. She pulled a phone from her pocket and dialled the number, but a message saying 'emergency calls only' flashed up.

The others all tried their phones but got the same message. "That's a bit weird," commented Rob. "Maybe it's the weather. The signal is usually great here."

"I need a wee," Ed was moaning.

"Go and get a bottle and hide in the corner," instructed Maria with absolutely no sympathy.

Marcus looked across at Merryn and Jamie who were holding on to each other and looking terrified. "What's up, you two? Anyone would think this place is haunted. Hey, it's not, is it? Oh, wow. A night in a haunted house...okay, building...Cool!"

Merryn and Jamie could not answer. Jamie had also felt the drop in temperature and was aware of a feeling of hostility creeping around them. They knew that they had to get out, but they couldn't; there was no escape. Merryn felt a faint scratch at her leg, and saw Galaxy whimpering at her feet. She sat down on the floor, leaning against a wall and the puppy buried herself tight into her lap. Jamie collected a sleeping bag and wrapped it around himself and Merryn.

"It's like we were tricked," whispered Merryn. "It made the building all safe and welcoming, then it captured us here. It's not over. It's coming back for us. You feel it too. I can see it in your face." Jamie wanted to say something consoling but he couldn't. He felt weird. His stomach was somersaulting and he felt like he was going to be sick. He thought back to everything Merryn had told him and he suddenly believed her. There was a voice in his head telling him that it all made sense now; Merryn was right. Something was going on and he did not like it one bit.

The eerie silence was broken by Ed. "What shall I do with my bottle?" The others groaned and called him 'disgusting' amongst other things. Once the bottle was placed right at the bottom of a bin bag, he joined the larger group commenting loudly that he did not want to be with the 'puppy love' group in case they did anything gross like kissing. That idiotic speech earned him a couple of slaps from Lily and Maria.

Rob, Ed, Marcus and the girls settled into their sleeping bags, not too concerned about being locked in. As Lily pointed out, they had food leftovers, drinks and no parents to tell them to keep the noise down. So they followed Rob's lead and decided to tell each other fantastical ghost stories.

Merryn and Jamie managed to ignore the giggles and chatter from their friends. Instead they attempted to find logical reasons for the situation. But no matter how hard they reasoned the underlying feeling was nagging at them. They had been set up. The freak torrential rain, the veil of welcome that covered The Assembly Room and now their imprisonment. Something had wanted them here but why?

22

The watcher was there as the doors opened to admit the witch hunter, his assistants, the accused and the braying crowd from the village. With shocked disbelief, she saw her companion watching too. How had he got there? It was her dream, wasn't it? She wanted to ask him why he was there, but, as always, she was struck dumb. He looked as bewildered as she felt, and attempted to go towards her. Confusion flooded his face when he discovered that he could not move. He tried to talk but no sound could be heard. He looked at her as if to ask for an answer. She could only reply with her eyes, and the look read, "We are helpless."

The prisoner was in between Goody Mills and Goody Phillips, her arms grasped tightly. Like Alice Wright, she was old, with grey, thinning hair and a spine that had started to curl over so she shuffled in a hunch. There were warts on her face and on her bare arms. Below her meeting eyebrows, she had the fire of hatred in her cloudy eyes. She was led to a chair at the end of the room facing the door, and her guards took their positions at either side. Edward Parsley stood about four metres away from the woman to mark where the crowd could stand while John Stearne placed himself behind the woman facing the crowd.

The watcher studied the crowd as they came in, pushing and jostling for the best position. There was the farmer who had betrayed Alice Wright, and there were his two sons who had drowned her. With Master Stirman was another man who looked awkward, and stayed on the edge of the group. She started in horror as she caught sight of some familiar faces, and turned to catch her companion's eye. By his expression, the watcher knew that he had seen them too. What was going on? Why were there so many people from her real life here?

Ed, Rob, Marcus, Lily and Maria were at the very front of the throng yelling 'witch' and screaming for justice. But they looked different. They wore the clothes of peasants. The girls were dressed in long black skirts, with white blouses and waistcoats and their hair was held back in a scarf. The boys were wearing long tunics and legging-style trousers with slipper-like shoes. They were dirty, and when they opened their mouths to yell, the watcher could see black marks where decay had claimed many of their teeth.

"Ladies and Gentlemen," John Stearne announced with his trademark flourish, as the room fell silent. "I am here to carry out the work of God, and cleanse this town of evil spirits and witches who will do the devil's work. This woman here, Goodwife Anne Cricke, is accused of using witchcraft against an animal. Let us hear her story before we decide whether she be tried as a witch.

"Goodwife Cricke," he continued. "Did you ask Master Waspe, the farmer, for eggs?"

Anne Cricke looked at the witch hunter and sneered. "Of course, I did. He is a farmer and he has eggs."

"Yes, but did he deny you those eggs because you could not pay him?"

"He does not need the money. I am starving. I have no money to buy eggs but he has a lot of money. He sold things from the church before they could take them away and destroy them. Don't think I don't know, Gentleman Waspe as you call yourself. I see these things." The man who was standing beside Master Stirman shuffled and stayed silent. But so many others heckled the accused witch that his guilty stance went unnoticed.

"And when he denied you those eggs, did you return and put a curse on his pig? Did you curse it so that its skin would bleed and blister? Did you force Mr Waspe to cut his pig's ears off and burn them just to lift the curse?" The witch finder continued, his voice booming from beneath the disguise of his hat.

Goody Cricke laughed – an evil cackle. "You are as daft as he is. His pig caught mites. And his pig caught mites because he keeps his pigs in dirty, stinking places. I told him his pigs would catch mites if he did not look after them properly. But he would not listen to a foolish old woman like me, he said. He knew what he was doing, he said. And one of his pigs died." She laughed again, then turned and spat in the direction of farmer Waspe.

"Are you confessing, Goodwife Cricke? Did you consort with the devil to kill this pig?" The witch hunter remained calm, knowing that the old woman was incriminating herself with each word.

"I am confessing nothing. I told that stupid man how to look after his pigs, and I told him he was greedy for not giving me any eggs. That is my confession."

"So you are confessing. Tell me, how long has the devil been with you?"

Anne Cricke roared with laughter. "The devil is not with me any more because my husband is dead. He died twenty years ago and I am really pleased about it. And no one has been with me since then; no person and no devil. And no-one is going to be."

"What about your imps, Goody Cricke? How long have your imps been coming to you?"

"What is an imp? I have never seen an imp. I have no imps. I have no animals. It is just me in my house by myself and I don't need anyone, especially not this lot," she replied gesturing to the silent crowd who could smell success.

"You say you have no imp, Goodwife Cricke, yet what is this on your head? Is it not an imp?" In a lucky break, John Stearne had spotted a fly on her head.

Anne Cricke became concerned suddenly. "What imp? I said I have no imps."

"And there is another," he continued as another fly landed on her shoulder. He would not admit to the onlookers that the flies were merely attracted to her strong unclean smell. In any other situation, she would have brushed them away without a second thought but she couldn't as her arms were tied to the chair. *"And another..."*

Suddenly, Lily screamed from the front of the crowd, "The imp has flown to me!" *She began thrashing at a fly that was buzzing around her. In her mind, however, it was not an insect; it was a flying beast. Maria was following her frantic movements and started joining her friend in howling at an unseen attacker. Soon all the villagers were getting dragged into the hysteria. They were brushing non-existent bugs from their hair and arms. They imagined they felt the creatures creeping inside their clothes and writhed around to rid themselves of the imps that were crawling across their flesh. The watcher saw Lily and Maria claw at their faces, leaving deep scratches. She saw Rob, Ed and Marcus duck their heads as they imagined they heard creatures from hell flying towards them. Over this hysteria, the woman was shouting, "I have no imps. I am not a witch."*

In a loud, authoritative voice, John Stearne spoke and immediately the townsfolk listened. "Please leave the hall. This woman is clearly in need of further investigation. For your safety, please leave." Instantly, the mania stopped and the crowd obeyed.

Merryn and Jamie woke up suddenly, though they had not remembered going to sleep.

"Did you dream what I dreamed?" Merryn whispered in horror.

Jamie looked at her and nodded his head slowly. He could not find the words to speak because nothing he said would make any rational sense. How could he talk about what had just happened without sounding insane? "Yes, I dreamed what you dreamed. We just saw the first trial of a witch from hundreds of years ago. Oh, and, our best mates were there. Isn't that cool?" Jamie imagined the conversation in his head and shuddered.

He put his arm around Merryn and hugged her tightly. It was easier than talking about what had happened. Because how could they talk about something that could not possibly have happened?

23

"Sleep well, folks?" Matt asked as he walked backwards through the door to The Assembly Room carrying a tray of tea, toast and bacon rolls.

"How did you get in?" gasped Merryn.

Matt looked at her, bemused. "Through the door. It's got this weird thing called a handle that you have to turn, then the door opens."

"Ha," replied his daughter. "We couldn't get out of there last night because it was jammed shut."

Matt clearly thought that this was an excuse to have a sleepover in that building. "So why didn't you phone me?"

"None of us could get a signal on our phones!"

Her dad looked down at his own mobile phone. "Funny thing, that. I've got a full signal on mine and I am on the worst network in the whole world."

"You don't believe me, do you?" Merryn sulked.

"It's true," Jamie said. "Even Ed couldn't get the door open."

"Well maybe the doors got swollen because of all the rain and got stuck," suggested Matt still not believing the pair of them.

To change the subject, and to avoid having to listen to any more feeble excuses about why the kids decided to sleep in The Assembly Room, Matt asked them all about the party. Merryn and Jamie were keen to put the events of the previous night to the backs of their minds, so they chattered away with as much fake enthusiasm as they could dredge up. They were so manically loud that they woke up the others. Matt decided to leave them to tuck into their breakfast. On his way out he called back, "Do you want me to leave the doors open? It's lovely out here." Merryn and Jamie shared a look. The freak weather that had changed the party plans just turned even more freakish.

"How long have you two been up?" yawned Rob.

"Not long," replied Jamie. "How did you sleep?"

"Like a log. In fact, I slept so deeply that I can't even remember falling asleep. The last thing I remember is listening to Lily's rubbish ghost story about the haunted moustache."

"That's a true story," retorted Lily. "I slept amazingly well too – a bit surprising considering this floor is so uncomfortable."

Marcus, Ed and Maria all agreed with her. None of them mentioned having a strange dream involving witches. "Mind you," added Maria, "those flies were a bit annoying. Did you hear them?"

Merryn and Jamie listened to their friends agree about the flies that had suddenly appeared and irritated them, then just as quickly vanished. Merryn could not understand what had happened. The others had definitely been there; she had seen them. But unlike her and Jamie, they had no memory of it at all.

Half an hour later, The Assembly Room was empty again; with the friends back in their own homes and Merryn sitting in the back garden in the glorious sunshine. She was fussing Snowdrop while Galaxy chased butterflies around the buddleia bushes.

"Did something go wrong last night?" Rosie's gentle question burst in on Merryn's thoughts.

"No. Why?"

"You just seem a bit down. Everything is okay with Jamie, isn't it?"

"I'm just tired," Merryn sighed. "I didn't sleep too well."

"That's nothing new," her mum laughed. "You just sit and rest out here. I've got to get on with a bit of studying."

Merryn watched her mother walk inside and fell back into her troubled thoughts. She should be so happy today. She felt like the luckiest girl alive to have a boyfriend as lovely and caring as Jamie. The party was a fantastic success. Plus she had a puppy to love and nurture. But she was scared. Last night's dream had been different. How could her friends have ended up in there jeering for justice? How could Jamie have been there watching with her? And when would this nightmare end?

She knew that the records showed only two Hitcham witches, and that there was no evidence that they had been hanged. But would she have to experience Anne Cricke's suffering too?

There was no more time for brooding as Merryn was called to fulfil the birthday duties and visit her great-aunt and cousin Ruby. Galaxy came along for the ride too, which pleased the energetic puppy, but really annoyed the house-proud relatives. It was highly amusing watching the great-aunt flinch every time the puppy came anywhere near her.

That evening, Merryn declared that she needed an early night and crawled in to bed after a long soak in the bath. She was exhausted and within seconds her eyes were drooping in heaviness.

24

A couple of hours later, Rosie looked in on her daughter before she went to bed. She was puzzled to see Merryn's duvet thrashing frantically as though the girl was moving her legs back and forward. "Are you alright, Merryn?" she whispered. There was no response, just the constant leg movements. Rosie stood and watched, waiting for the bizarre activity to stop. But it didn't, and Merryn did not seem to wake up.

The following morning, Merryn shuffled downstairs to the kitchen table. She looked pale and weary, yawning constantly.

"What's up, love?" asked her dad.

"I don't know. I am absolutely shattered but I think I slept okay. And my legs are killing me – I feel like I've run a marathon."

"Are you okay to go to school today?"

"I have to," yawned his daughter. "I have a Maths' test. Don't worry. We weren't meant to study for it."

Matt was not convinced that Merryn would cope with a day at school but did not push the point. He was right. All day long, Merryn was restless. In lessons, she fidgeted constantly; at break times, she paced the field. There was not one moment when she was actually still. She got several detention warnings for her inattentiveness throughout the day, and all her friends found it funny to mock her restlessness.

Only Jamie was worried. He kept asking her what was going on but she could only answer, "I don't know - I just can't keep still. I'm so tired. I want it to stop, but it won't."

After the bus deposited Jamie and Merryn at their houses, he insisted on escorting her to her door. As she walked away, too restless to return his farewell hug, Jamie spoke in a hushed whisper to her mum. "She's been like this all day – she won't keep still."

"She was bad last night too," commented Rosie. "She was asleep but kept on moving all the time. I don't know what is up with her. Maybe she got overtired and will just crash. Don't worry, she'll be okay."

Jamie smiled and shouted 'see you later' to Merryn then trailed back to his house miserably. He felt useless.

The pacing continued throughout the evening and by night-time, Merryn was walking a course around the house and garden. She would follow the walls of a room, move on to the next one, out into the garden, then repeat the process again. On several occasions, Rosie saw Merryn's eyes droop and she would stumble, then she jerked upright again as though she had been poked in the side.

Rosie kept begging Merryn to stop, but her daughter wailed, "I can't. I have to keep moving but I'm so tired. Make it stop. Please make it stop." Matt tried to physically restrain her, but she just fought against him. Her parents were at their wits end and had no idea what to do.

The walking continued during the night and into the next day by which time Merryn was knocking her swollen feet into furniture and crying in pain. Rosie and Matt kept Merryn away from school, and sought advice from their GP who was as baffled as them. When Jamie dropped by to see her after school, he was horrified by what he saw.

Merryn walked around the lounge, dragging her feet as though she had lead weights tied around her ankles. Her face was grey where the tears had forged a track down her cheeks. She kept mumbling to herself; words that Jamie could not work out. Knowing that he could not stop her, he held her hand and walked with her. She looked at him and whispered, "Help me. I'm so tired. Make it stop," but kept on moving.

The third night of her pacing saw Merryn add the perimeter of The Assembly Room to her route. Had she not been so exhausted, she would have noticed a face at the window following her movements. She would have realised that it was a different face from before but with many similarities. It was an old woman again, but this one had a look of hatred and defiance rather than despair.

Suddenly, exactly three days after the walking started, it stopped. Merryn collapsed in a heap on the lounge floor and screamed, "I'll confess". Then she fell into a deep, still sleep. Matt lifted her up onto the sofa and left her there.

The watcher knew that she was dreaming again, but it was different. It was as though she was watching a summary of Anne Cricke's trial; the edited highlights, or 'the best bits'. The pricking trial seemed to be over in a flash, but she still saw the carefully chosen audience assemble, and she despaired as she realised that the modified tool was to be used again.

Another flashback followed and the watcher saw John Stearne address the audience outside The Assembly Room. "I have worrying news for the safety of your village. The devil has such a strong hold over the woman in there that she will not answer our questions. I am forced to use persuasion to get to the truth. For that reason, Goody Cricke will be walked for three days and nights."

Anne Cricke laughed when she was told of her latest punishment. "You are making me walk? For what purpose? I walk all the time. Do you think I will confess because you make me walk? When do you want me to start?"

The watcher felt as though she was on some roundabout. She saw the start of Anne Cricke's trial, then she saw flashes of the rest of it and all the while, her head was pounding with dizziness. Instinctively, she knew how far through the trial each episode was. How she knew this was wholly inexplicable, but she had learned to accept the illogical in these dreams.

At first, the old woman coped extremely well. Anne Cricke began pacing The Assembly Room early in the morning, muttering obscenities and firing looks of hatred at the witch hunter and his assistants as she passed them. Then, the watcher's vision blurred. When she re-focussed, it was the evening of the first day. Anne Cricke stumbled as she walked past the door to The Assembly Room and struggled to get up. John Stearne allowed her a minute to sit on the floor until he demanded that she move. "Well, old woman. You lasted longer than I expected. Enough rest now. Goody Mills, help the lady up." Anne Cricke glared at him and quickly got to her feet. She did not want any witch finder's assistant touching her any more.

The watcher's head spun as she saw flashes of the woman's progress through the night. She saw Anne Cricke's pace slow more on each occasion but she kept going. For the next day and night, the watcher saw her shuffle and trip her way through the long hours, crying in pain but refusing to submit.

At one point, he returned after a rest in his rooms. "You could confess, Goody Cricke. Then I will allow you to stop and go to sleep," John Stearne offered with a silky tone in his voice.

"I will not confess lies," she hissed defiantly. "I am not a witch."

And so it went on. By the end of the third day, Anne Cricke could barely take a step without howling in agony and stubbing her swollen feet against the walls. Eventually, she collapsed on the floor and screamed using the last vestiges of power in her body, "I'll confess!"

Merryn did not wake up from this dream, but had anyone been watching, they would have seen the streaming tears and heard the heart-wrenching sobs. On her feet they would have seen blisters, grazes and blood; marks that would disappear within minutes.

25

Merryn slept for fourteen hours, and woke at seven-thirty on Thursday morning. She dashed around getting ready for school, despite being told to stay at home by her concerned parents. Jamie was amazed to see her running for the bus half an hour later, and he felt himself grinning like an idiot.

He could not believe that this was the same girl who had looked like a walking ghost the last time they had met. This girl was his Merryn, and he hugged her tightly in case she transformed back into the monster.

At lunchtime, they made their excuses to their friends and walked away together. Ringing in their ears were good-natured taunts about true love and 'needing to be alone'.

Merryn told Jamie all about her dream; the walking torture of Anne Cricke and her decision to confess. In turn, Jamie told her all about the walking nightmare from his point of view. "It's almost like you were possessed," he suggested, turning slightly pink as he said such a ridiculous thing.

"That's what it feels like. Sometimes, anyway. Usually I just watch, but I've suffered with them too. It's like they are deciding what they want me to see, but they're making me feel the pain too."

"Who are 'they'?"

"The accused witches," Merryn replied calmly, as though their conversation was as normal as a discussion on 'The X-Factor'. "Watching was a trial too, wasn't it? They would watch the witches till they confessed, spy on them, stalk their every move. Does that mean I'm doing the trial too?"

Jamie could not answer the inexplicable, so he did the next best thing. He put an arm around his girlfriend, and they sat in blissful confusion until the bell for afternoon lessons rudely interrupted them.

Walking back into school they decided to find out as much as possible about the history of The Assembly Room and Merryn's houses. Merryn and Jamie had to endure a barrage of teasing when they walked into registration. Wolf-whistles, kissing noises and questions about the date of their forthcoming marriage filled every available sound wave in the room. Even their teacher teasingly reminded them not to hold hands in the corridor.

After an afternoon of similarly infantile behaviour, the couple spent the evening huddled over the laptop in Merryn's bedroom frantically researching. Rosie helped by providing not only the lasagne and coke, but also by handing them a large box full of documents.

"We found these in the cupboard in our bedroom when we moved in," she explained. "I haven't had a chance to look through them yet though, but there might be something interesting in there."

As Rosie was leaving the bedroom, Galaxy nearly knocked her over in her own haste to get out. The puppy sat on the landing, whimpering, but refusing to be enticed back in. Meanwhile, Snowdrop pushed the opposite way and starting rubbing her head on the dusty old box, purring deeply. "Those animals are nuts," Rosie laughed as she went downstairs.

"Galaxy," coaxed Merryn repeatedly. It was no use. The dog would not go to her mistress. In fact, she lay with her paw flung over her nose and her eyes tightly shut. "Jamie. Do you think she's okay?"

Jamie looked across at the shivering little heap on the floor and also called to the dog. "She's probably just sulking because Snowdrop is there." Merryn looked at the cat and mentally agreed with Jamie. Snowdrop was slinking round the room, rubbing her head on the box and purring louder than the engine of a sports car. Her reticent, antisocial pet suddenly decided she wanted attention. If only those pets could speak.

The Internet did not help very much in their search. They learnt that The Assembly Room had been used as a reading room, a village meeting place and a place of worship at different times since the mid 1800s. Before that, no electronic records existed.

"That would fit in with the building," Jamie commented. "It is very Victorian in the way it looks, with the Gothic arched windows, the brick chimneys and the slate roof. Yes, I know I sound nerdy," he added when he saw Merryn's look of gob-smacked astonishment.

"Sorry. I'm thinking of being an architect, like my Granddad. Anyway, these houses must be from the sixteenth or seventeenth century. It says here that, if you had money but weren't rich, your house would be half-timbered and you'd put wattle and daub between the wood – whatever that is. But, if you were rich, you had bricks in the gaps. You had slate on the roof if you were middle or upper class, and thatch if you were a pauper. Mind you, these houses are semi-posh because you have chimneys instead of a hole in the roof like the paupers would have had."

"So whoever lived here to begin with was fairly well off but not rich," surmised Merryn, grinning at her boyfriend's geek-like waffle. "And how come this house was done up when the other one wasn't? Plus who added all the anti-witch charms, and when?"

Jamie shrugged his shoulders and held out his arms to take hold of the top half of a small pile of extremely dirty documents that Merryn was holding out to him. Snowdrop went to sniff at his pile then turned away in disgust. She headed for the pile that Merryn was holding and started rubbing her head and purring.

The documents Jamie had were old but not ancient. He found some architect's plans that showed the addition of Merryn's upstairs bathroom and the change of the walls downstairs. That was dated from the 1950s and bore the name 'William Stearne'.

"That's a bit creepy!" he shivered.

"Not really," answered Merryn. "That must be my dad's Grandfather. Dad inherited this place from his uncle, John Stearne – yeah, I know, great name – but he spent most of his life in hospital. William could have been his father."

"You could be right. I've just found a will from 1957." Jamie ploughed through the legal speak and beautifully formed handwriting. "Here we go - all my worldly goods and chattels shall go to my son, John William Stearne. No mention of a wife or any other kids. Is there anything in your pile?"

"Not really. There's some stuff that looks like guarantees and bills of work for the bathroom and the kitchen. Looks like they were done in the 1950s. There's an old parish magazine from June 1958. Usual church service information...oh hang on...there's an obituary of William Stearne. Apparently, he was born, bred, married and died in the village. He was born in 1901, only had one child, John William Stearne, wife died in childbirth, worked as a clerk for a solicitor in Stowmarket. Oh this is interesting," Merryn read aloud. "He had a deep fascination with the occult, particularly with witchcraft. He wrote a lot of papers on the subject but they were all destroyed. He fought in the Second World War, and eventually died from tuberculosis."

As Merryn lifted the next piece of paper, Snowdrop jumped at the pile, sending them everywhere. Once they were scattered, she rummaged purring deeply. Suddenly she bent down and grabbed something in her mouth. Merryn tried to prise it from her but Snowdrop responded with a hiss and a scratch.

"She's got a comb – a really, really old comb. Ugh, it's still got some white hairs in it." Snowdrop stalked proudly out of the room, then sat on the landing. She started licking the comb, then rolled over it as though it was covered in catnip.

What was perhaps more disturbing than the behaviour of this temperamental cat, was the apparent age of the comb. It was not made from any man-made product – it was as though it was fashioned from bone. Yet the hairs looked like they were freshly fallen from a human head.

26

"If anyone finds out what we're doing, we will be called geeks for the rest of our lives," Jamie commented as he and Merryn walked into the records office in Bury St Edmunds the following morning. It was a Saturday, and their research had proved disappointingly dismal. One search had thrown up this place, so they begged a taxi-ride from Rosie and decided to research some archives.

The overpoweringly helpful woman on the desk exacerbated this new found nerdness. "How splendid it is to see youngsters wanting to find out about their local history. We don't usually get people your age in here."

She soon stopped being quite so enthusiastic when they told her what information they were after. "So, you want to find out the history of those two cottages and The Assembly Room in Hitcham because you want to find out about witches? Shouldn't you be going to the museum?"

After assuring her that they were headed there next, Merryn and Jamie giggled as she went in search of the catalogue numbers. "Does she think we are going to set the forces of evil on her, or something?" sniggered Merryn.

"No, we're going to try her as a witch! Just don't tell her your surname." Unfortunately the woman returned just as Jamie was saying that and she glared at the teenagers. She shuffled her rather large frame to a microfiche viewer in the corner of the room, expecting them to follow. They were not treated to her customary offer of further help.

The records office was a lot more helpful than the Internet. Within two hours, Merryn and Jamie had discovered that the two cottages passed into the ownership of a Mr John Stearne in the months of May and June, 1645; their previous owners had been Mr R Wright and Mr J Cricke. But there were no signatures of sale, just of ownership.

"Guess we know that your latest accused witch didn't come home, don't we?" Jamie sighed.

About a month after the property belonging to Anne Cricke had been signed over, there were tenancy agreements made on the properties to a Mr Smith and a Mr Waters. Following that there was no record at all of any transactions on the houses.

"So what does that tell us about the houses?" Jamie sat back and took his eyes away from the screen.

"That those houses have been in my family for centuries," replied Merryn, "and that after John Stearne was given them, he stuck tenants in there. And there is no doubt I am related to John Stearne."

Jamie looked at Merryn with immense sympathy. "Just because you are probably related doesn't mean that you are the same as him. My great-grandmother ran away to Paris so she could be a dancer at the Moulin Rouge – can you see me wearing feathers and doing the can-can?"

Merryn smiled ruefully. "I'd rather be a can-can dancer than a murderer."

Jamie turned back to the screen and began hunting for anything to do with The Assembly Room. Once again, the information was sparse but very useful. "There's loads of stuff after about 1840," he reported. "It seems that someone called Reverend A Stearne from Lawshall, near Bury St Edmunds, applied to have the place rebuilt. Oh, that's interesting! It was in a state of dereliction and total disrepair following extensive fire damage. He applied to use the place as a community hall for 'general meetings and worship'. Wonder when it was burnt down.

"At the same time, he applied to update one of the cottages – the one you live in – but not the other one. Maybe he ran out of money."

"Great. So I have a witch hunter and a priest in my family tree," muttered Merryn. "Can you have a look to see when it burned down?"

Jamie had to dig way back. There were no official documents regarding The Assembly Room before that point, but eventually he found an ancient log from parish records.

"I may be a genius," he declared, "but hold on to your applause until I tell you what I've found. There's a report in a parish log from October 1645. A local man returned from fighting in the Civil War because he was injured. He had been presumed dead. Anyway, the first thing he discovered was that he was homeless because there were tenants living in his house and someone else now owned it. Secondly, he found out that his mother had been tried for witchcraft and died in prison."

Merryn had put her own misery to one side and felt an intense pity for the stranger. "Whose son was he?"

"Just a minute. He was so angry about the way that the villagers had treated both his mother and the other accused witch that he set fire to The Assembly Room. In his defence, he said it was to stop any other innocent, old women suffering in the way that these two had. He was found guilty at the assizes, sent to Colchester prison and died there of cholera."

"So it was Anne Cricke's son."

"Yes. John Cricke burned The Assembly Room to the ground and it looks like no-one touched it since; not until John Stearne's relative turned up to claim his inheritance in the early Victorian times."

"Do you want to find out anything else?" Jamie asked a shell-shocked Merryn.

"I don't know if I can cope with knowing any more," she answered. "And I don't blame you if you don't want to know me any more. It can't be much fun for you going out with a freak. 'Hey, guess what? My girlfriend's great-great-great-whatever was one of the Suffolk witch hunters!' That will do wonders for your social standing."

Jamie laughed and hugged Merryn reassuring her that he didn't care. That show of affection earned a glare and a loud tut from the woman at the desk, so they decided that it was time to leave.

27

It took the watcher a while to work out where she was. It did not help that it was pitch dark except for a small window high up in the wall allowing in just a crack of light. Even that, however, was covered with bars.

She worked out that she was in a room – perhaps fourteen feet long by eight feet wide. There was another window between this room and the room next door. That was another small space, but perhaps wider than this room. There was no light in there at all. Outside both the rooms was another chamber. It contained a great fireplace that had not been lit for a very long time and a huge wooden wardrobe. There was a thick oak door studded with nails leading from that into the inner realms of the castle.

The watcher had visited this place on a school trip and she recognised it as the prison of Colchester Castle. Before her eyes could become accustomed to the dark, her sense of smell took over. She smelt the stench of human waste, dirt, illness and damp, and her eyes stung with the strength of the mingled odours. Even in the other-worldliness of dreams, she wanted to gag and vomit out the taste that clung to the back of her throat.

She heard noises too. There were murmurs as the prisoners spoke to one another; hushed murmurs in case they incurred the wrath of the gaoler and a subsequent beating. There were rustling noises as prisoners shuffled around the damp straw on the bare stone floor, as well as groans of despair, pain, and countless wheezing coughs.

The watcher wanted to cry for pity. The whole place felt as though it was only one step away from death, and an air of defeat hung low over the inmates.

She was inside one of the two cells, but, again, no one knew that she was there. The gaoler approached the bars that were fixed on a large window next to the heavy, impenetrable door. He held up his light, obviously alerted by some over-loud whisper, and it gave the watcher a chance to look around. There were about thirty women in this room; most of them huddled together at the walls. They were shackled either at the hands or feet, although some seemed shackled at both.

"Hush that noise!" the gaoler yelled, banging at the bars.

"She is ill, Sir. She needs help," returned a voice from the women's cell. The watcher recognised that voice as belonging to Anne Cricke, although it was changed. Gone was the mocking, defiant tone she used to goad the witch hunter; she spoke with acceptance of her fate and weariness of the world that had cheated her.

"Stop your ranting, woman, or it will be another trip to the oven for you."

The watcher saw Anne bow her head in submission. She knew that the old woman did not want to return to 'the Oven' – a cramped, windowless hole in the ground, in which prisoners were left for twenty-four hours as punishment for whatever act the gaoler deemed worthy of further degradation.

"Do not try to help me," a pitiful voice rasped. "I am not much longer for this world. Then I can go and return to the Lord. That will show them that I was not a witch."

Anne Cricke's patient was obviously dying. There was a smell of vomit about her and, had it been lighter, the watcher would have seen the dried smears of blood on her chin. The hard, burning lumps that were on her neck, under her arms and on her inner thighs would have shown up black under natural light. Anne was rubbing the woman's legs to soothe the aching muscles. In a couple of days, the woman would die a painful death from the Bubonic plague.

The watcher looked around at the other women scratching away the fleas that had carried in this terrible disease. They also itched from the lice that carried the typhus. So few of them would eventually make it to the assizes to be tried – maybe that was a blessing.

Through the hatch separating the rooms, she could see that the men had not fared any better, although they were fewer in number. They too scratched, ached, coughed and prayed for an end to their suffering.

"Why are you here?" the woman asked Anne. "You said your family is not from here."

"It matters not where I am," Anne replied. "I have no family. My husband is gone and my son is dead in the fighting. I am here because they would not take me to Bury St Edmunds. It is full, I believe."

"Full of other innocents!" interrupted another prisoner.

A man from the neighbouring cell joined in the conversation. "They are afraid that if they get too full, we will revolt against them and escape!"

Anne laughed, "Like we can run quickly in these shackles."

They fell silent as the gaoler approached with his light, threatening the 'Oven' and 'Little Ease', another punishment involving the prisoner being detained in a high alcove reached only by a ladder. So the watcher heard no more from the prisoners. She did, on the other hand, hear a conversation between others.

"I'm here to see a prisoner, Sir," announced a deep, authoritative voice. "A Rebecca West."

"I am sorry, Sir," replied the gaoler, Stephen Hoy. "She is a 'close' prisoner. I cannot allow you to see a witch for fear that she will try to send her evil spirits to taint your soul."

"Hold up your light, Sir, then answer my request again."

The gaoler held up his light and a face could be seen. Under his brimmed high hat with the cylindrical rise ending in a flat circle, was curled hair falling to the man's shoulders. He had a beard that came to a point past his chin. He dressed as though he had money, wearing boots, a cloak and a leather jacket. He had the air of correctness, but there was a touch of evil around his edges.

"I apologise, Mr Hopkins, I did not see that it was you under this darkness. I will fetch Mistress West."

Merryn woke up with a start. So that had been Anne Cricke's fate: imprisonment in Colchester castle before a trip to the assizes. But to be stuck in such horrendous conditions without knowing that her son was actually alive? Death would have been kinder.

28

Merryn woke up the next morning with a slight headache. Despite four hourly Paracetamol attacks, it remained a dull ache for the day. Still, she managed to get on with her homework in the morning and go to the cinema with Jamie in the afternoon.

They made a vow not to discuss anything to do with witchcraft all afternoon and it worked until they got back. Getting out of Mr Foster's car later that evening, Merryn raised the subject when Jamie walked her to the door.

It was still light outside as it was only the beginning of July, but the moon was also hovering over The Assembly Room. "It's horrible to think of what they did in there," Merryn pointed to the building as she said this.

"We don't actually know that anything did happen in there," reasoned Jamie.

"Of course it did. I was there. I saw it and so did you."

"It may have only been a dream," Jamie continued knowing that he really should stop before he caused an argument.

"How can you say that? Especially after everything we've been through." Merryn made to go to her door, but Jamie grabbed her arm.

"I'm sorry. It's just that the more I think about it, the more I realise that it cannot be happening – or that it shouldn't be happening."

"What about what I've seen? What about everything I have felt? Explain why people right next door to The Assembly Room had to stuff their walls full of witch charms to keep themselves safe. Explain why I know things that aren't in the books. Tell me how I know that Anne Cricke was sent to a prison in Colchester Castle. How do I know that she looked after another prisoner who was dying of the plague? What about everything we found out yesterday?"

"I'm not saying that there weren't any witch trials here; there were, and there is loads of historical evidence to back it up. And there's evidence of witches in Colchester Castle – maybe you just added Anne Cricke there in your mind. Maybe your imagination is getting carried away. I mean, all this haunted stuff – isn't that all a bit 'Paranormal Activity'?"

Merryn was looking at Jamie as if he was a stranger. "So I made it all up? Is that what you are saying? Who have you been speaking to?"

"Well, Rob was round this morning and I told him a few things..."

"Great. So now you and your best mate think I'm a lunatic. Thanks for nothing, Jamie. See you later."

Merryn pulled out of Jamie's grip and marched to her front door. She slammed it as he tried to follow, so he had to walk home forlornly. Jamie knew it hadn't been right to talk to anyone about Merryn's apparent hauntings, but he needed someone to talk to. He was finding it hard to accept what was happening and he thought that his friend would understand. He should have known better. The only advice he got from 'the expert in women' was that Jamie really needed to pull Merryn out of her self-deluding belief in ghosts or dump her. All Rob had achieved was to make Jamie feel stupid at believing in ghosts and lose him the best girlfriend he had ever had. Some best friend.

He sulked home, then went straight upstairs. He saw that Merryn was on-line as soon as he went onto 'Facebook', but she ignored his appeals to talk. Why had he not followed his gut instinct about the haunting and not listened to his friend? Because he could not totally believe his gut instinct – that was why.

"Are you alright Merryn?" Rosie yelled up the stairs. She guessed that there had been a bit of an argument as her daughter had stormed straight up the stairs even ignoring Galaxy. The puppy had to settle for sitting outside her favourite person's bedroom door, dropping the toy she brought for her mistress against the wood, and making an occasional whimper.

"Yeah. I've just got a bit of a headache, so I'm having an early night." Merryn opened her door to collect her furry companion, then slammed it shut. It was true. Her headache would just not shift, and she had blackened her room as much as possible because the light seemed to be making it worse. Merryn decided that it was probably just a migraine brought on by the stress of an ignorant boyfriend, or maybe an ignorant ex-boyfriend.

She lay under her duvet, cuddled up to her canine hot water bottle and fell asleep.

The watcher could see Anne Cricke sitting on the floor in that same awful cell. Even though it was pitch black, she could see clearly this time. The smell had got so much worse; even the gaoler seemed to have covered the lower half of his face with something resembling a handkerchief.

Anne was leaning against a wall with her legs outstretched. Resting in her lap was the woman she had seen previously. Anne was stroking her hair and singing nursery rhymes.

The woman looked terrible. The lumps on her neck seemed to have burst and were now covered with dried pus and blood. Her eyes had lost their glow, yet they were alive enough to allow tears to gently drop onto her cheeks. She took a sharp breath then turned to face Anne.

The watcher heard her last words. "You are a good woman, Goody Cricke. Thank you." And then it was all over.

Anne leant over the woman and whispered. The watcher concentrated and could just hear that she was reciting the Lord's Prayer, before adding a final prayer of her own begging for this wretch to find peace in heaven.

When she had finished, Anne shouted. "Gaoler, there's another for you. She's dead."

Within ten minutes, the gaoler had brought in a large sack and ordered the prisoners to put the body inside. Then he picked it up and carried it away as though it were nothing more than a piece of rubbish.

The watcher wondered whether he would put the body somewhere safe so that a post mortem could be carried out, and a verdict of 'gaol fever' recorded. Or whether the body would merely be burned, as was usually the case with plague victims.

Before the dream faded, she heard the voices of both women and men praying together for the soul of the dead woman.

Merryn woke up briefly with the words of an incantation echoing around her brain. She couldn't quite work out what was being said, but it was soothing. As she turned to sleep on her other side, she winced at the shooting sparks of pain erupting in her head.

29

Waiting for the bus that morning was extremely awkward. Jamie had spent the previous evening and night feeling guilty for doubting Merryn, but he could not forget Rob's warnings of how stupid he would look when people found out about his girlfriend's beliefs.

Merryn felt angry with Jamie and disappointed that, after all their investigating, he felt the need to err on the side of logic. She could not bring herself to say anything other than 'good morning' to him, then chose an empty seat at the front of the bus. Her headache had got so bad that she could not face a confrontation with him.

Following her mum's advice, after ignoring her suggestion to stay at home, Merryn was alternating Paracetamol and Ibuprofen every two hours. It took away the shooting pains but the dull ache remained, distorting her vision and causing lights to flicker in front of her eyes.

She muddled through the school day and spent her free time in the library, attempting to get on with her history project. But the words blurred and the harsh lights seemed to bore into her brain. No one really noticed, though. The gossip-mongers were too bothered expressing concern for the state of her relationship with Jamie to see her pain. They attributed her off-handed rudeness to anxiety over the impending split up.

Dan Wesson, a swaggering example of someone who fancied himself as the best asset to the female population at school, received the worst of Merryn's wrath. Never one to worry about stepping on the toes of good taste or sensitivity, he sidled up to Merryn in their Maths lesson.

"I'm really sorry to hear about you and Jamie," he injected even more syrup than usual into his bee-snaring voice. "But he was never good enough for you. You need to find someone who will treat you right."

By this point, Merryn had added nausea to her headache complaint, and was beginning to believe that she would shortly follow through. "Can we have this conversation later, Dan? I'm not feeling too good."

He placed his hand on her shoulder in what he had read in his sister's magazine was a gesture offering compassion and understanding – something a caring boyfriend would do. "I understand, Merryn. It is difficult going through a break up. But you are handling it so well."

Merryn could feel the sick rising up from her stomach to her throat. "Dan. I really do need to go."

But he increased the pressure on her shoulder, forcing her to duck from beneath his grasp. That was all it took. As she turned to attempt to make a dash for the toilet, she lost control. Merryn vomited all over Dan's brand new 'Vans' trainers and spattered the pressed creases in his freshly laundered trousers.

While the teacher sent for help and emptied the recycling bin to use as a sick bucket, the rest of the class fell to the floor in hysterical laughter. The girls who had previously faced humiliating rejection from Desirable Dan revelled in his downfall, and the boys (including his friends) who had always been made to feel inferior, enjoyed their moment of smugness. Even the teacher silently appreciated that it could not have happened to a better person.

In fact, by four-thirty that afternoon, Merryn had become something of a Facebook hero. She did not feel heroic, however. After being taken home by her father, Merryn fell into her bed and stayed there for the next three days.

With the sickness came a high temperature, aching joints and diarrhoea. The advice that came down a telephone line was to have plenty of fluids and rest. Pretty standard stuff really.

Merryn was awake for the first day and needed the comfort that illness craves; although Snowdrop, her generally constant bed companion, refused to go anywhere near her. Even Galaxy kept her distance but that was more down to her mistress's inability to throw toys to fetch. That evening, Merryn gave in to sleep.

The watcher was back at Colchester Castle, back in the prison. It was still full of women, but a lot of the faces were unfamiliar. Whether they had gone to the assizes or whether they were still alive, she had no way of knowing.

Anne Cricke was there. The fight had left her long ago and it was obvious that she was losing a lot more than that. She was hunched against a wall with her eyes closed. The watcher knew that she was awake as her breathing was rasping and occasional sharp cries of pain emitted from her mouth.

Is it death that is meant to be the great leveller? Anne Cricke was certainly about to lie amongst fellow accused witches and the gentry. But it would be her shadow that joined them. The Anne Cricke of Hitcham who would annoy her neighbours with her rude behaviour; who would pester and goad people until they gave in to her demands; who dared to defy John Stearne until she collapsed from walking; that Anne Cricke was gone.

Anne's eyes started to flicker. Suddenly they were wide open and she was staring straight at the watcher. There was a message in that look but the dream faded before the watcher could decipher it.

By the third day of her illness, Merryn was lapsing in and out of sleep. The dreams had become part of her reality and she found it difficult to remember where she was when she woke up.

The doctor's advice continued to be one step away from useless. It was only when Merryn started hallucinating that a home visit was agreed. She woke up screaming at Galaxy on the afternoon of the third day. "Get away from me, imp. I will hang and it is all because of you. Get this imp away." She was still cursing the imps when the doctor arrived.

Within thirty minutes, Merryn was sitting in her dad's car being rushed to West Suffolk Hospital in Bury St Edmunds.

Her temperature had reached forty degrees Celsius, and she was clearly dehydrated. What caused the panic, however, were the strange lumps appearing on her neck, under her arms and on her inner thighs. In fact, those lumps earned Merryn the exclusive temporary address of the isolation ward.

No one would tell Matt and Rosie the suspected nature of Merryn's illness. That was because they were not prepared to accept the fantastic truth, and they would not dare to believe it themselves before more tests. The doctors and nurses had never actually seen a case like this, although they had heard about it in their studying. They were almost excited about treating their first case of the Bubonic plague.

30

The watcher could see that Anne Cricke was still there. She was in the same position; crouched against the wall, her neck angled at one side. She had raised her skirt to allow the cold of the stone floors to soothe her burning legs. Her cheek rested against the damp wall, but she soon evaporated away the moisture.

The lump on her neck was as large as an orange but a lot darker. The blackness seemed to be spreading across the rest of her skin, leaving her looking like an enormous bruise. She sat muttering. Those close to her heard the words of 'The Lord's Prayer'; those too far away heard the babbling of a mad woman.

Merryn started muttering in her sleep. It was now the fifth day of her illness and she was getting worse despite the powerful intravenous antibiotics. The medical staff felt helpless as they debated different treatments. Although the case made fascinating viewing, watching a real person suffer in such a horrendous way made them feel sick to the core. And they had absolutely no idea what to do for the girl.

"What's she saying?" asked one nurse through her face-mask. She was standing beside the bed changing the bag of fluids.

"Nothing that makes sense!" answered the other nurse, carefully positioned at the foot of Merryn's bed.

"No, listen...she's praying. It's 'The Lord's Prayer'. Can't you hear it?"

"You're hearing things. Come on. Let's get out of here – I don't want to end up looking like that!" The second nurse left hurriedly through the door to the anteroom, leaving the first nurse gazing in pity at the child.

She must have been so pretty a few days ago. But now... Not only was she gaunt and pale, those lumps that seemed to be expanding every second were becoming darker. The nurse felt tears prick at the back of her eyes and she sniffed back her sympathy, telling herself harshly not to get involved.

"How is she?" asked an exhausted Rosie as that nurse came through the anteroom.

"I know the doctor saw you earlier and, medically, there isn't much more to add. She's still asleep. There is something strange, though." The nurse did not want to raise the parents' hope but she had to tell them about the praying. "Are you religious?"

Matt sighed, "Is it time to pray for a miracle?"

"No, no, no, I didn't mean that at all! It's just that Merryn was mumbling in her sleep. She was saying 'The Lord's Prayer'."

"We're not religious," Matt answered. "She'll have learnt that at primary school. I've never heard her use it, though. Was she awake?"

"No. It was like she was sleep-talking."

"That's a good sign, isn't it?" Rosie was grasping at any faint hope. But she lost her grip when she saw the nurse's face fall. "It's not a sign at all."

"I'm really sorry, Mrs Stearne." Matt and Rosie did not see the tears re-appear in the nurse's eyes as she turned away.

But they did see a sheepish-looking boy turn the corner of the corridor accompanied by his mum and dad. And they saw him pretend to rub his forehead so that his tear-filled eyes were hidden. The adults did not speak a greeting, but hugged and cried together.

Jamie went to stand at the window to the anteroom and peered through to Merryn's bed. He gave way to his misery as he looked at the tubes and wires attached to his beautiful girlfriend. He tried hard not to look at the lump under her neck or the discoloured skin around it but it was impossible. It looked like something out of a movie about demonic possession. He continued looking as the parents stopped sobbing and discussed Merryn's condition. Then, not caring how ridiculous he sounded, he began to talk to Merryn through three panes of glass.

"I'm sorry about the flowers – I mean not bringing any. I wasn't allowed to bring them on the ward. I wanted to bring you an i-Pod, but I'm not sure that would be allowed either. They might have wanted to sterilise it or something. My mum washed mine a month ago and it's only just recovered.

"You won't believe how much people at school love you. Dan Wesson looked such an idiot and no one will let him forget it. Did you know that Jasmine got it all on her phone? And she's put it up on Facebook. There's even a club started up – you know, one of those 'I like' clubs – and it's called 'Merryn Stearne the Legend'.

"Merryn, I'm so sorry that I didn't believe you. I shouldn't have listened to Rob. I've done a bit more digging and I found out that Anne Cricke ended up in Colchester Prison and died of the plague. But I suppose you already know that, don't you, or you wouldn't be here. Please get better, Merryn. I really miss you."

He had to stop talking because of the choking tears. But he did not stop watching the steady rise and fall of her chest. It was lucky that he did carry on watching. Had he stopped, he would not have seen what happened next.

Merryn's eyes opened wide and she turned her head ever so slightly; just enough for her to make eye contact with her boyfriend. Jamie was too hypnotised to move or speak.

She did not make a noise, but her eyes told their own story. She looked at him with a desperate smile; a look of forgiveness; a look of elation at seeing him. The look quickly changed to despair and her lips began to move. He could not make it out and he mouthed back, "I don't understand."

Merryn kept mouthing the same two words again and again until he repeated them. "Help her?" The look in her eyes changed to gratitude and she shut them gently.

That broke the spell. "She was awake!" Jamie yelled. After that, the room was full of white coated, masked people coming and going, speaking frantically.

Fifteen minutes later the prognosis was given. Jamie must have been mistaken. Merryn was deeply asleep; there had been no change in any of her graphs or charts. In fact, she had slipped into a coma.

31

Today must have ranked as one of the worst in Jamie's life – so far.

The news from the hospital was not good. Merryn remained in a coma and was fading away before the watchful eyes of her parents. The enormous abscesses were starting to burst and the medical staff now had the danger of septicaemia to add to the list.

Everyone who had been in contact with Merryn had been tested for signs of the plague, but no-one at all showed the faintest trace; not even Dan Wesson. A few enterprising students, however, read up and rehearsed the symptoms just to miss school.

Merryn's pets were flea combed and treated with rigour to eliminate them as the carriers of the disease. Their coats had been clear. All those who were looking for a medical explanation for the source of the plague were baffled. Jamie did not attempt to enlighten them. How would that sound to rational people? My girlfriend caught the plague from a witch who lived in the 1600s – perhaps not the most believable line.

Jamie experienced a highly emotional moment when he handed in Merryn's history project. "It's not finished," he apologised to Mr Carter. "But it's really good and she worked really hard on it."

"Would you like to keep it so that Merryn can finish it when she comes home?" the teacher offered quietly.

"I think she'd want you to read it, Sir," replied Jamie. "Though I'm not sure that you'll believe it."

"This is powerful reading. Do you believe it?" It had looked like Mr Carter was only going to skim read the essay, but he did not put it down until he finished.

"Yes, I do. At first I thought she was mad, then I changed my mind and I believed it. Then I changed my mind again and nearly got dumped, but now I do – one hundred percent."

"Incidentally, where did she find all her evidence? I don't remember reading about all of this when I did my research."

Jamie went silent and looked at the floor, kicking away at an imaginary scuff mark. He knew that he was going to sound stupid so he took a deep breath before answering, "She sort of dreamt a lot of it."

"Ah, that explains it." Mr Carter was looking worried now. "The link between Merryn and her ancestors must be pretty strong. You don't need to feel foolish for admitting to a belief in the supernatural – I won't tell anyone, so long as you don't tell anyone that I believe in all that too. Do you know that quote from Shakespeare's *'Hamlet'*?

There are more things in Heaven and Earth, Horatio,

Than are dreamt of in your philosophy.

It's worth remembering that, Jamie."

By now, Jamie was wishing for that much longed-for hole to magically appear and swallow him whole.

"Did you find out where they were buried?" Mr Carter asked.

"No," Jamie replied, relieved that the conversation had taken a more realistic turn. "Alice Wright was definitely buried in Hitcham church, but Merryn thinks they might have put her with the paupers and there's no sign of a headstone. There're no records of Anne Cricke. In fact, there were no official records of her even being in Colchester Castle."

"That's because she should not have been sent there," replied the teacher. "John Stearne had got carried away with his own power by that point and was sending far too many innocent women and men to the assizes. He probably took her to Colchester as Bury St Edmunds wouldn't have accepted her on his flimsy evidence. I doubt that there are any records about where her body went after her death."

The bell rang for the next lesson and Jamie turned to the door. As he turned the handle, Mr Carter called after him, "Following the Salem witch trials in America, a plaque was erected to pardon the witches. It was both a memorial and an apology. Something to remember."

Jamie hurried out and bumped into Rob. "What were you doing in there?" he asked. They fell into a conversation about

Merryn, but Jamie could not push away Mr Carter's final remark about the plaque; maybe that would end the haunting. He couldn't see, however, how a simple sign made from plywood would appease a vengeful spirit. It was worth a go, though – anything was, if it would save Merryn.

One of Jamie's major talents was art. So the 'simple sign made from plywood' became something of a work of art.

He shaped it like a gravestone with a Gothic, ornate arch on the top. Using thicker pieces of wood, he created a 3-d effect. Then the whole piece was sprayed with grey paint, and edged in thin lines of black interspersed with a fleur-de-lys pattern.

The writing was done in a Gothic font, and was amazingly beautiful. He was unsure about what to write in the centre but eventually settled on this:

In Memoriam of the Hitcham Accused,

Alice Wright and Anne Cricke.

Tried, Tortured, and Died in 1645.

Remember their lives, not their deaths.

The next problem was where to put the plaque. Jamie debated whether to talk to the local vicar and arrange for a ceremony in the church. But he settled on displaying it where the haunting seemed to have begun – The Assembly Room.

Two evenings after his discussion with Mr Carter, Jamie had just been given the latest news on Merryn. She was still deep in a coma and the abscesses were now starting to burst. He was not allowed to see her as her appearance would have been too upsetting for him, but his parents continued to go, just to support Matt and Rosie.

Jamie did not want to upset Merryn's parents by talking about death, albeit deaths from hundreds of years ago, so he took steps to display the plaque by himself. The Assembly Room door was unlocked and it creaked in resistance as he heaved it open. The air was cold, despite the continuing heat wave, and it seemed to be pressing in on him. As he walked around looking for the best place to mount the plaque, he wished that he could ignore the whispering voices that hissed at him to get out.

Suddenly he felt pressure on his back. It was as if he was being shoved forwards. Jamie stumbled towards the door, then felt the invisible hands again. That was all he needed and he hurried out of the building, still clutching the memorial.

Merryn was still foremost in his heart and motivation, which was lucky as his head was telling him to run. He watched as the door shut behind him then he smiled in relief as he found the perfect spot. The plaque had two short feet, which he dug into the hard ground next to the step outside the front door, underneath the left-hand window.

Jamie did not know what he expected, but he had hoped for some reaction. However, there was nothing; no evil shadows screeching out of The Assembly Room, no sudden feeling of calm and tranquillity, no sign of any exorcism. Maybe it would take time. Maybe it would make no difference at all. Desolately, Jamie returned home to wait by the telephone.

32

The watcher was there as the prisoner breathed her last breath. Anne Cricke had not moved at all during her final two days, although her fellow prisoners checked regularly for signs of life. She looked as though she was in some sort of half-life. She did, however, become animated just before she died. About one hour before the end, Anne started talking constantly. At first, it was thought that she was ranting; however it soon became apparent that her words made sense.

Her eyes were wide and excited as she talked of her son being alive and coming back to cleanse the evil wrought by John Stearne. Then she began insisting that the other one was coming closer and he would kill many. Anne kept repeating the date 27th August over and over again. Her third topic of conversation was that the people of Hitcham now knew the truth. They had proved that they recognised the real devil by honouring the accused.

However lucid the words were, they sounded scarily like prophecies. The other women desperately tried to hush her in case the devil was trying to get to them through her words.

They did not have to worry for too long on that matter. On 5th July 1645, Anne screamed a howl of gut-tearing pain, then stopped breathing. Strangely, her face did not stay in a death mask horror. Instead, she looked wholly at peace with the faintest smile tugging at the corners of her lips and her eyes closed as though in a contented sleep.

Suddenly, Merryn let out an ear-piercing scream. It sounded as though she was being ripped apart inside; so horrific was the intensity. The scream went on for at least five minutes, enough time to allow the room to fill with white coats and nurses' uniforms.

Matt and Rosie held each other and wept. They truly thought that this was the end of their little girl. The Fosters were also weeping and clutching hands, hardly believing that such a gregarious, beautiful child could be gone. The wait for the news seemed to be never-ending. In reality, it was only thirty minutes later that the troop of doctors and nurses filed out of the room leaving two nurses with Merryn and a doctor to face the parents.

"Mr and Mrs Stearne, I have some news for you," the doctor announced with a quiver in her young voice. She was only just out of training and she had never had to do anything like this before – probably never would again either.

Matt and Rosie could not bring themselves to look at the doctor, so the Fosters spoke for them.

"Has she gone?" Jane whispered.

"Er...no," came the astonishing reply. The Stearnes had expected to hear the word 'yes' and did not acknowledge the opposite. But Jamie's parents sparked up.

"No? You mean that Merryn is alive?" Nick gasped. Now Matt and Rosie were listening, with faint smiles waiting to be given permission to break through the tears.

"Yes, she's alive. She seems to have made a miraculous recovery that has baffled us all. Do you want to see her?"

There was no need for an answer. Merryn's parents burst into her room and nearly fainted in surprise.

Merryn was sitting upright in her bed, all the tubes and wires removed, taking small sips from a cup of water. She smiled when she saw her parents. "Didn't think you could get rid of me that easily, did you?" she grinned and welcomed their enthusiastic hugs.

After a new wave of tears was spent, Merryn asked, "Is Jamie here?"

Jane, who had been standing in the doorway, answered the question. "He's on his way now. His brother's driving him over, and he's really looking forward to seeing you."

The doctor took Matt over to one side and attempted to explain what could not be explained. "Mr Stearne, I don't know what to say to you. But I will have a go and I apologise in advance if it upsets you." The doctor waited for a sign from Matt and he nodded for her to continue.

"Obviously you heard that scream. While she was screaming, the abscesses burst. I shouldn't say this, but we thought that was the end. However, as they burst, the colour of her skin changed right before our eyes. You remember that her skin had started looking a sort of liver colour because of the septicaemia? Well, the discoloured skin starting dissolving from the outside in – a bit like a back to front ripple. Normally, we would have expected the abscesses to remain as open sores, but they closed up and fresh skin seemed to form while we were watching her. It was the strangest thing I have ever seen."

The doctor stopped and took a long swig from the water bottle she was carrying. She hoped that her patient's father believed at least some of this as she could hardly believe it herself. But he seemed to be bearing up, although he looked shell-shocked.

"After her skin cleared up – and that was all over by the time she finished screaming – she just lay there for three minutes. In that time, she didn't move and her pulse remained slow and steady like she was still in a deep sleep.

"But then, she sat up. She just sat straight up and yawned. I know how crazy this all sounds, Mr Stearne, and I don't blame you for being sceptical..."

"Please carry on, doctor. At the moment, I will believe anything. We've been going through so much weird stuff in the past few months that this isn't too far from our reality."

The weary half-smile on his face convinced the doctor that she was not talking to a mad man, so she continued. "We were amazed that she sat straight up. Remember that she's been laying flat on her back for six days, and she got up with no dizzy tinge or headache or anything. We took her temperature, which had been at nearly forty-three degrees prior to the scream. It had gone back down to thirty-seven degrees. All her muscle movements are back to how they should be. She has no symptoms at all. In fact, anyone visiting her now would call us liars for saying that she had the Bubonic plague."

"But is she really okay?" Matt asked.

"See for yourself," shrugged the doctor. They turned to look at

Merryn, who had just beamed as Jamie walked through the door with a goofy smile on his face.

"What about side-effects?" continued Merryn's dad.

"We don't know yet. Usually, the side effects from the Bubonic Plague are what you might anticipate with blood poisoning – like gangrene, infections and such-like. Also, you would expect severe drowsiness, maybe nausea, diarrhoea and dehydration. Most of the side effects come from the drugs.

"In Merryn's case, we just don't know. She is a little dehydrated and could do with some good meals to get a bit of flesh on her bones. But other than that, we will have to wait and see. She won't be allowed home for at least three days because we want to monitor her, run some tests and make sure that she is all right.

"Your daughter is the luckiest patient I have ever heard of, and I am so pleased. Someone, somewhere has obviously been looking out for her. Maybe she has a purpose in her life; some sort of destiny that needs to be fulfilled." The doctor blushed and Matt took hold of her hand with tears in his eyes again.

"Why or how she was saved is irrelevant. My daughter is alive and that's all that matters. You and your team have been wonderful," Matt said. Then the doctor left the room and made a phone-call; she had a sudden urge to speak to her little sister, who just so happened to be Merryn's age.

33

As it turned out, Merryn had to stay in hospital for a day longer than anticipated. Two days after her illness miraculously vanished, she was preparing to go home. All the tests and observations showed a healthy, normal teenage girl. There was not a single trace of her disease; at least, that is what the doctors agreed.

Merryn lied to them. While her recollections of her own suffering were blurry, she remembered her dreams of Anne Cricke in terrible detail. She could see the broken, poisoned body of a woman who had lost the fight against the plague. And she could remember her prophecies: Anne's son would return, something would happen on the 27th of August and the people of Hitcham would forgive the accused witches.

The first and last statements were a puzzle to Merryn, but the second was scarily familiar. August 26th 1645 was the date of the assizes court in Bury St Edmunds in which eighteen accused witches had been sentenced to hang. It was not until the following day, however, that their punishment was served. Perhaps Anne Cricke had possessed 'witchly' powers of fortune telling.

On the night before she was expected to return home, Merryn went to bed with her presents and cards packed in her bags. She was soon sleeping, though not peacefully.

The watcher saw the young man ride into the village one July evening. He rode up to the door of a house just behind The Assembly Room and stood on the threshold. "Mother! I have returned!" he yelled. There was no answer, so he limped through the cottage and into the kitchen.

It was changed. The large wooden table had been scrubbed and fresh flowers were on top. The place was clean and tidy, not at all how his mother kept her home.

Suddenly, the back door opened and a young woman walked in with two small children trailing behind her. She screamed.

"Who are you?" the man and the woman shouted in unison.

"Where's my mother? What are you doing in her house?" he asked. He tried to remain calm because the two little ones were looking terrified and clinging to their mother's skirt.

"This is my house. Me, my children and my husband live here; not your mother, whoever she may be."

The man guessed that his mother must have died. He had been away for a long time, battling in the war, being injured and then fighting for his life as he recovered from the wounds to his legs. He wobbled a little as he tried to keep his balance, and the woman took pity on him.

"Sit yourself down before you fall on my clean floor. Then you can tell me who you are looking for. Simeon, go and fetch your father from the field," she continued.

The largest child ran quickly from the room, pleased to have an excuse to leave. The man lowered himself into the chair.

"Now, tell me who you are looking for," the woman demanded still standing close enough to the door in case she needed to escape.

"My mother lives here; or maybe she used to live here," he mumbled.

He told her that his name was John Cricke, that he was raised in this house alone, his father having disappeared when he was a baby. His mother told people she believed that he had gone to fight the cause with the early revolutionaries, but he knew that he had gone as far as Stowmarket and a widow named Goody Stewart.

John went to fight in the troubles when he was nineteen – two years previously. However, he had been left for dead in a battlefield eight months later, then taken in by a kindly old woman and her husband. He recovered, mostly, but he was left a cripple and found it difficult to walk. Eventually he was strong enough to return home.

"What is your mother's name?" asked the woman picking up a milk jug to put on the table.

"Anne Cricke," he replied, and the woman dropped the jug. The noise brought her husband hurrying in from outside.

"Who are you? What are you doing in my house?" the husband yelled, ready to hit the stranger.

"He's a cripple," hissed his wife, *"and his mother was that witch."*

John Cricke looked at her in horror and total misunderstanding.

"Did you not know?" the woman questioned holding back her aggressive husband. And so the tale of Anne Cricke's demise was told to her only son. The woman could not tell him whether or not she was still alive, only that she had gone to Colchester prison.

The man struggled to his feet and stumbled to the door. He climbed back on his horse and rode in the general direction of Colchester. *"Do not return!"* shouted the husband. *"It is our house now. You have no claim. Who would want this place anyway?"* he continued, speaking quietly to his wife. *"I don't want this haunted pile. We are only here because the rent is a peppercorn. Who wants to live in a witch's house?"*

Two nights later, when the darkness had finally triumphed over the pushy summer sun, the man returned on his horse. This time he did not go to the house. Instead he headed directly for The Assembly Room, but no one saw him come. He was not seen as he stumbled around the field at the side of the building collecting grass that was dry and brittle. Nobody noticed that he bundled piles of this grass against the door. He blended into the darkness as he lit a reed torch with a flint and flung it into the thatched roof. The thin lines of smoke went unseen and the crackle of flames went unheard. A second torch was thrown into the pile at the door. Within minutes, The Assembly Room was engulfed by fire.

Only then did the couple stir and run from their house. They were powerless to intervene. The stream that ran alongside the land, and the pond behind The Assembly Room had run dry weeks ago. The straw in the thatch was so brittle that it lit like tinder.

The noise of the flames drowned out the jubilant words of the man riding away on his horse. *"That is for my mother. Never again will you murder an innocent woman!"*

Merryn woke up screaming those very words, thus denting her chance of leaving hospital without further tests. They would want to know that there was no medical reason for her outburst.

There was, however, another reason for her delay in returning home. That same night, The Assembly Room burned down.

34

"Matt, something's wrong." It was the middle of the night and Rosie was nudging her husband awake.

She had heard a noise outside, a rustling and some crackling. She could have sworn that she had also heard horse hooves, but that could not have been possible. There was a smell, too, and a vague flickering light.

As Matt stirred, Rosie's brain began to wake up. "Matt, something's on fire!"

Rosie jumped out of bed and hurried across to the bedroom door. It had been left open since Merryn went into hospital so their daughter's restless pets could wander the house looking for her. The house seemed to be okay.

Then she walked to her bedroom window and looked out in the direction of The Assembly Room. Flames were licking out of the windows and smoke was billowing through new holes in the roof.

"Matt!" she screamed. "The Assembly Room is on fire!" That woke him up.

Rosie ran downstairs to dial 999, and Matt put on his jeans. He dashed outside but realised that he was helpless. By this point, Jamie, his brother and his parents along with their other neighbours had joined Matt in feeling useless.

The Fosters could only offer comfort as they invited Matt, Rosie and the pets into their home in case the fire spread further. Snowdrop refused to budge from Merryn's bed, swearing and hissing, but Galaxy thought it was time for adventure.

The fire brigade came within ten minutes and spent the next three hours getting the fire under control. At five o'clock in the morning, Matt talked to the leading fireman. The building was no more than a shell. Although the walls were intact, they were not safe and could collapse at any minute. The roof had fallen in a long time ago and nothing remained of the wooden struts and beams. If it was a car, The Assembly Room would have been a write-off.

"So you have no idea at all about how it started?" Matt said.

"We're baffled," was the answer. Matt had come to loath that word. "There is no sign of anything obvious. The experts will come tomorrow to investigate but the only strange thing we found in the wreckage was a bit of flint. Actually, there was another thing, but don't ask me to explain it. We found some weird plaque just by the front door. Look."

The fire fighter returned with a beautifully crafted board that was singed at the edges with the top layer of varnish bubbled away. The words that Jamie had painted on there were still clear. "You can keep that bit of miracle, mate," he offered. "I still don't know how that thing avoided going up in smoke; the doorway was one of the hotspots. What's that quote about there's more things on heaven and earth? Anyway, good luck with it all."

Matt stood staring at the remains of his dream as everyone left. He was cursing his bad luck and thinking of everything that had gone wrong since he inherited these places. He lost his job and couldn't get another, Merryn looked like she was going mad, then nearly died from the Bubonic Plague and now this. In a fit of paranoia, he felt as though he was being punished for something.

Matt broke the news to Merryn the next morning but did not receive the reaction he expected. There was no shock, horror, surprise or even concern. She already knew that The Assembly Room had burned down despite the nursing staff being told to keep the news from her.

Instead she began preaching, "It was a place of evil and the only true way of purging evil is by fire. That was what happened last time. John Cricke burned it down in 1645 to cleanse the evil and to stop them trying any more witches."

"What are you talking about now, Merryn?" Rarely did Matt lose his temper with his daughter, but he could not handle her strange behaviour right now.

"I am talking about the witch trials that they held in there, back in 1645. They tried two witches in The Assembly Room and they both died, although neither of them was hanged. Their names were Anne Cricke and Alice Wright."

Matt felt sick. Those were the names on that wooden plaque. What on earth was happening to him, to his family?

"They want you to stay here tonight, Merryn. We don't know how safe everything is at home yet, and apparently you had a bad night."

"It's safe at home now, Dad. But I don't mind staying. Jamie said his brother would bring him over later if I couldn't come home. Don't worry. I'll be fine."

But Matt was worried. He was very worried and he had a horrible feeling that he had only just started to scratch the surface of his worries.

Since switching to online bank statements several years ago, Matt had ceased to study and scrutinise his bank balance every month. In the glory days of a London weighted salary, they had no money worries. They were not extravagant but they did not need to scrimp on the weekly bills. Unfortunately, when the job situation changed, their lifestyle did not.

A quick online check the other day showed an alarming lack of funds in their account. They had enough to live on for the next three or four months but after that; they would need to get an income from somewhere. Either that, or hope that the other cottage would sell quickly.

He would have to finish it first though. All these recent dramas had put the renovations behind schedule, and now with The Assembly Room being nothing more than smouldering rubble, who would want to buy a period cottage with a view of that?

And now his daughter was acting like a mad person. All her talk of witches brought back memories of his lunatic uncle. That would be just his luck – a rogue gene of insanity that chose to reappear in one of the precious people in his life. Look how that had turned out for Uncle John. He could not bear to think of Merryn ending up the same.

35

Merryn was laughing with Jamie and Galaxy in the back garden. The school year had just finished and the sun was still beating on the baked ground. To an onlooker, it was a tableau of an optimistic piece of happy poetry. Behind the scenes, there was a different tale to be told.

Matt and Rosie were busy with yet another estate agent in the cottage, who was repeating the same rubbish. "Lovely house, blah, blah, blah, superb renovation work, blah, blah, blah, unpredictable housing market, blah, blah, blah, won't sell until The Assembly Room is repaired."

As soon as he left, Rosie dashed out to start her evening shift at a supermarket in Stowmarket. She had been lucky enough to land a night job re-stacking shelves; the money was okay and her colleagues were fun. However, the havoc it played with her sleep pattern was not so good. Matt felt guilty that she was doing it, but there was no choice.

Jamie and Merryn were watching Galaxy chase a butterfly, while Snowdrop observed from the safety of a high tree branch. "Merryn, are you really better now?" Jamie asked.

Her face darkened as a shadow passed over her. "I'm still having dreams," she confessed, "but they're different. They're not very long; in fact they're more like a snapshot. I keep seeing the same man riding a horse. He's not alone. John Stearne is just behind him, but he's more of a blur - like he's not so important. And I can't see the new man's face clearly. I don't know where he's going. I just have a feeling that he's coming closer to here. It's weird; it's like I'm watching stages of his journey. And it feels bad."

Merryn had gone quiet. "Bad, how?" prompted Jamie.

"Threatening bad, maybe – I don't know." Jamie did not ask

130

any more. It was clear that she was used to understanding what she had seen, and did not like the uncertainty.

With the destruction of The Assembly Room and the dream-death of Anne Cricke, Jamie hoped that Merryn would be free. He could not understand how the haunting was working. If either witch had possessed her, surely Merryn would now be safe. But he knew that there was more to it.

Merryn was being made to watch a story unfurl – that much he was sure of. She had been forced to see and experience the horror of the Hitcham trials but they were over, and there was no evidence of a witch finder returning to the village after those initial events. Jamie researched John Stearne's steps after his time in Hitcham to try and find some clues.

It seemed that the witch finder made his way to Wattisham village at around a similar time and tried at least one victim. Then he moved in a north-easterly direction through the county. He had a lot of success in Rattlesden; a place described as being crippled by poverty and hardship that had lost a great deal of its community to the Puritans in New England. This amazed Jamie. Rattlesden was such a picture postcard, beautiful, outwardly affluent village now.

When John Stearne turned up, Rattlesden was already under the spell of superstition because of the legend of the 'Black Shuck' of Clopton Hall. That was said to be a creature with the body of a monk and the head of a hound whose purpose was to guard a hoard of gold.

In August 1645, John Stearne sent five accused Rattlesden witches to the assizes in Bury St Edmunds: Meribell Bedford, Henry Carre, Elizabeth Deekes, Old Mother Orvis and John Scarp. It is possible that the two men died in gaol and Elizabeth Deekes was hanged. It was also said that a nine-year-old boy was tried for witchcraft there.

Following his triumph in Rattlesden, John Stearne rode to Wetherden where he set his sights on the happenings in the manor house at Haughley Park. At least two women were sent to trial from there. Through Haughley he continued and on to Bacton, where his witch finding skills were in great demand.

It was all very interesting but it did not explain Merryn's dreams. She said that there was another man and he was coming towards them. However, John Stearne had ridden away from Hitcham following the persecution.

"Hey, you two are not going to believe this," yelled Matt bursting into their thoughts. "I've just had an e-mail from the Lottery Grant people. I applied on their 'Village SOS' scheme to get some funding to rebuild The Assembly Room and they've approved it."

Merryn felt a sick feeling seeping into her bones. "What're you going to do?"

"They've awarded us enough money to do up the place and return it to community use. We're even going to be on the TV. They have to film us at different stages in the renovations to show the progress, and, yes, I will give you two a starring role. Isn't that great?" Matt expected elation; he got silence. "Well? What do you think?"

"We don't need it," said Merryn. "Hitcham already has a village hall."

"This is going to be more than a village hall. It can be a reading room, a venue for concerts and exhibitions, somewhere to meet..."

"Somewhere to hold trials!" interrupted Merryn.

"Get over it!" shouted her dad. "That was hundreds of years ago; if it ever happened at all. Will you just stop all your rubbish about witches. I thought you would have been pleased. We have a chance to give something back to this village and maybe save ourselves from ruin. Plus you get to be on the telly. And that is how grateful you are."

Matt stormed back inside feeling guilty for yelling at his daughter but also annoyed at her attitude. Just because of her hang-up with whatever happened in the past, she would not accept that the real world had to keep moving. That is, unless she could not separate the real world from the one that was in her head.

A few days later, Matt was awaiting the supplies to start work on The Assembly Room, along with the arrival of a volunteer work force. A television crew was due to turn up later in the day to film the first stages. However, that was the day the weather decided to change.

There had been months of sweltering heat – except for the freak rain in June – and there was no sign of a let up of the heat wave. But, on Matt's big day, it rained and rained and rained. Although it was the wrong time of year, it was the start of forty days and nights of teeming rain. It was so heavy that all work on The Assembly Room was abandoned. The supplies lay outside the shell, becoming more and more sodden and useless as the days passed. Once again, Matt cursed his luck and watched his bank balance continue its downward spiral.

36

The watcher saw them come closer. By looking at the landmarks - the river, the church of St Peter and St Mary, she could see that they had arrived in Stowmarket. Now she looked at their faces and recognised John Stearne. He was riding just behind another man whose face was not so familiar. That one was dressed as a gentleman in much a similar way and exuding an air of confidence. Then she realised. She had seen him in Colchester Castle. This was Matthew Hopkins – Witch finder General.

She saw them make their first stop at the parish church where they were warmly greeted by two official men, who introduced themselves as Thomas Young, the vicar, and William Manning, the churchwarden. The watcher chose not to listen to their conversation but she watched their expressions and body language.

Mr Hopkins and Mr Stearne looked earnest and humble as they explained their godly mission and the other two men looked grateful for the divine intervention. She wanted to yell at them not to listen; to learn from the horrors of the previous months, but, as always, she could not make a noise.

She did hear the witch finders' claim for payment. They declared that, usually, twenty shillings each would be enough to cover their expenses. However, they would have to ask for more if the evil proved more widespread. The church officials seemed less pleased about that, but they shrugged their shoulders and agreed.

Time shifts in strange ways in your dreams, and you are able to skip the less important parts. Therefore, the watcher was saved from having to watch Mr Stearne and Mr Hopkins find helpers from within the town to act as seekers. There was no problem in recruiting women willing to weed out the witches in their midst. Just like today, there would always be people desperate to get involved in any sort of drama – no matter what the potential outcome.

One of their first victims was Elizabeth Hubbard. As a trial, she was watched by Goodwife Cobbold and Goodwife Price of Stowmarket. Watching witches was not a furtive, undercover exercise; it was more like having an annoyingly devoted dog follow your every single move. Once at night, they heard her calling for her three children to come to her. That was all the evidence the seekers needed to bring their accused witch in front of the witch finders. Widow Hubbard had no children; they all died as infants and she blamed herself for their deaths. Matthew Hopkins declared that calling for the dead was the same as conjuring the devil, therefore the woman must be a witch.

The questioning continued, and Widow Hubbard soon confessed to malefaction in her own family. She claimed to have wished harm on her cousin who subsequently fell lame. Matthew Hopkins did not want to hear how her cousin had stolen money from her and caused her to fall into poverty. He did not care that the same cousin fell from a horse that she bought with money she had stolen, and her lameness was the result.

But as further proof to appease an assizes judge, Elizabeth Hubbard was weighed against the enormous, metal bound church Bible. It was believed that if the victim weighed less than the Bible, then she must be a witch. Months of near starvation meant that this poor wretch did not stand a chance. Such conclusive proof of her guilt ensured that she was hanged.

The seekers and finders did not rest there. They swept through the streets and eventually declared that seven men and women of the town were witches and would have to stand trial.

Soon, the watcher saw Mary Fuller in her small cottage in Combs, which is at the southern edge of Stowmarket. She was alone with no husband, and had nothing but a few cats for company. Her cottage was bare, dark and dismal. There was very little furniture; what she did have had been used for firewood. There was hardly any food in her cupboards.

She saw the witch finder's assistants follow Mary wherever she went. They watched as she walked to the orchard and begged windfall apples from the farmer, and saw her curse him as he refused her request. They watched as she picked blackcurrants from the brambles and stuffed them into her starving mouth. They watched as she returned home, angry, frustrated and hungry. They saw her curse the horse in the field opposite her home as it ate the windfall apples she had been denied.

And they returned the next day to see the horse lame.

The watcher saw Mary Fuller presented to Matthew Hopkins and John Stearne the following day at the Corn Exchange. Tied onto a chair with only the witch finders and his assistants for company, the questioning began.

"Widow Mary Fuller, you are accused of witchcraft. You have been seen to cause lameness in a horse after it ate the apples you were denied. How do you answer?" Mr Hopkins opened his questioning with his characteristic swagger. The woman paused before lifting her head and staring directly into her questioner's eyes.

"How should I answer? Shall I admit it and get the punishment over and done with? Or should I quake and cry and deny all charges so you can torture me? What would you do, Master Hopkins?"

The assistants looked at each other, waiting for their leader's response. Never before had he been challenged. They saw him shuffle his feet and straighten his shoulders.

"You must answer as you see fit, Widow Fuller. Do you wish to confess?"

The old woman smiled and licked her lips. "Hmmm. What should I confess to? I am a witch and I like to curse people who upset me. I am a poor, old woman who everyone hates and wants to see hanged."

"Are you confessing, Widow Fuller?" Mr Hopkins continued wiping his brow.

"Let me see," she said. Then she turned slowly to look at each person in the room. Afterwards, they all agreed that they could not find the right words to describe the look they had been given but agreed it had come from the devil himself. "I might be, I might not be. If I am a witch, then I will be able to escape from your torture, will I not? If I am not a witch, I will suffer for a while, then I will be released from this cruel world, will I not? You will be helping me either way, Master Hopkins."

136

"The evidence, Mr Parsley," demanded the witch finder. He snatched some papers from the outstretched hand of the clerk and took an inordinately long amount of time reading and re-reading them. All the while, Mary Fuller was humming folk songs and nodding her head in time.

"Widow Fuller," the witch finder continued. *"You demanded eggs from a farmer's wife, who refused you. That lady was then stricken with stomach pains and had to take to her bed. Your neighbour, Goodwife Farrell, would not allow you to take any milk without payment. That good woman later suffered a miscarriage. How do you answer?"*

Mary Fuller smiled a lazy smile. *"I am starving and I get upset when I am not allowed to eat or drink. Does that make me a witch, Master Hopkins? Do you have a wife, Master Hopkins? Would she help out a poor, starving, old woman? Or would she make her suffer?"*

The room fell silent and Mary smiled in triumph. *"Another one for the assizes, Master Stearne,"* Matthew Hopkins said and he swept out of the room heading straight for the nearest hostelry. Laughing in scorn, Mary Fuller was prepared for the journey that would take her to prison in Bury St Edmunds.

Suddenly, the dream went fuzzy and the watcher became disorientated. Instead of being a spectator, she was a part of the dream. She was travelling, seeing Stowmarket retreat into the distance. There was a heavy weight on her wrists and she looked down to see shackles. Her clothes felt wrong. They were heavy, made of some woollen material, and they were really old and smelly.

"It's Mary Fuller, isn't it?" a kindly voice next to the watcher whispered. *"Do you remember me? I am Mary Abbott. Your mother used to come and cook for us when I was a child – until we got sent to the poor house. We would play together, you and I. Do you remember, Mary?"*

The watcher realised that it was she who had been addressed as Mary Fuller. She felt a flicker of confusion until a stronger force stifled it. She turned to the old woman and glared. Fear plunged deep in the other woman's heart and she shuffled as far away from this hostile creature as possible.

Merryn woke up rubbing her wrists where she had felt the shackles. Her skin felt itchy where the wool had touched her, and a deep sense of despair hung heavy in her heart.

Fully awake now, Merryn knew what the next part of the haunting was all about. On 26th August 1645, eighteen 'witches' were condemned in Bury St Edmunds, and hanged the following day. It was one of the most famous of all the witch trials and perhaps the most horrifying.

She must do something. But what could she do? It had already happened and there was nothing she could do to alter that. Even if she had access to the Tardis and all the trickery offered by the Doctor, she would be helpless.

Suddenly a thought caused her blood to run cold. Tomorrow or today (depending on what time it was now) was the 26th August. She had to go to Bury St Edmunds. She may not be able to help but the least she could offer was a bit of solidarity.

But was it just that? Merryn felt as though there was no choice, that she must go - no matter what. It was as though she was being pulled there, like she had to answer a calling.

She texted Jamie. "I know it's the middle of the night. Sorry. Do you fancy a trip to Bury tomorrow?"

A few minutes later, she got a reply. "Thanks for waking me up at 1.30am! Okay. Go to sleep. See you later."

37

"Remind me again, in case I didn't understand. I didn't get much sleep cos someone woke me up at some stupid time in the morning," Jamie dug at Merryn as they sat in a train on the journey from Stowmarket to Bury St Edmunds.

"It's the 26th of August," explained Merryn inexplicably.

Jamie waited for a real explanation, but it did not come. "And?"

"And," she replied as condescendingly as possible, "August 26th 1645 was the day that eighteen witches were convicted and sentenced to death. On the following day, they were hanged."

"Back to my question. And?" repeated Jamie.

"And I needed to come here to pay some sort of homage."

"Merryn, that was about three hundred and sixty-five years ago. And where exactly are we going? You keep saying there are no records about where the trials or hangings happened."

"I'll know when I get there," was the only reply that she would give.

Jamie knew the futility of arguing with his determined girlfriend so changed tack. "At least promise me that we can go to MacDonald's when we get there. I'm starving."

Merryn smiled and her boyfriend saw a glimpse of the girl he liked; the one who was frivolous and fun, not the one who was so deeply immersed in her obsession with witchcraft. He wished the whole drama would be over, as he did not know how much more of this he could take.

They got off the train at Bury St Edmunds and walked down to the exit. Jamie headed off to the right expecting Merryn to be following him, but when he turned to ask her a question, she was not there. Merryn was still outside the front of the station, looking around. She was so lost in her thoughts that she did not respond to his shouts of, "Come on, Merryn, you promised me MacDonald's."

Instead, she turned to the left away from the town centre. Jamie yelled again to unhearing ears, then realised he was wasting his breath and followed her. He had absolutely no idea where they were heading. There was nothing over this side of Bury St Edmunds other than houses and car dealerships.

Glad that no one they knew could see them, he caught her up and they walked together in silence. They turned to the left, and walked under the train bridge, then turned left again up a road called Thingoe Hill. On the left hand side of the road were large detached houses, while the A14 took pride of place on the right. Jamie was so bemused that he forgot his hunger temporarily.

"There was a hill here though they called it a mound," Merryn announced as though she was reading from a textbook. "And this road would have joined up to Northgate Avenue, which is just the other side of the A14. They hanged the witches on the hill. In 1645, eighteen witches were hanged on that hill. And what is there left to remember them? A noisy, dirty, smelly motorway."

He opened his mouth and tried to find something intelligent to say, but all Jamie could manage was a sort of 'huh' sound.

"They took them to the assizes at Shire Hall on Shirehouse Heath; not the new Shire Hall near the brewery, but the old one on another mound, Henhowe it was called. That's gone too. They tried them, found them guilty and took them to sleep in a barn overnight. Then they brought them here and hanged them."

Looking around, Jamie found it hard to believe that anything so sinister could ever have happened here. Beyond the houses was a gym and some industrial units: all the evidence of a normal, uninspiring twenty-first century lifestyle. But he had experienced enough recently to realise that nothing could ever be taken at face value. Perhaps that is why he did not question where Merryn's knowledge came from.

Merryn was still lost in her thoughts, although she seemed to be returning to the world of reality. Then she turned to Jamie with a look of despair on her face. "Why am I here, Jamie? Why did I think that I'd come here and find some miraculous answer?"

Jamie so nearly answered what he was really thinking. "You came here because you're losing it. You're living in a mad world of witches and ghosts. I really care about you but you are doing my head in."

Instead he took a deep breath. "You found their hanging ground. You didn't know where that was until you got here. You kept telling me that no one seemed to know. So maybe that was your purpose for coming: to see where it happened."

"I don't understand, though. I don't feel anything. We're here, right where they were murdered but I can't feel them."

Again, Jamie was lost for words. Thankfully, Merryn carried on. "Right, enough of our wasted trip. I believe that you, too, have had a calling. MacDonald's, wasn't it?"

So they turned round and set off back towards the town centre, Merryn trying hard to be lively and chatty. She thought that she would come here, be lead to the hanging hill and find an answer. Maybe then it would all be over. Instead, she found even more questions. It had gone on long enough - the visions, the dreams, the suffering and the haunting. Merryn wanted them to point her in the right direction, so she could give them the solution they wanted and get on with her own life.

Jamie saw the hurt behind Merryn's frivolity, and felt guilty for feeling annoyed at her. He had no idea what she thought she would achieve today; all he knew was that it hadn't worked. Almost telepathically, he was thinking the exact same things as his girlfriend. Jamie wanted to shout at the ghosts to 'bring it on and get it over with'; then maybe they could both move on.

Although unease tapped at the back of their minds, the couple spent the rest of the day in a light-hearted mood. Jamie got his MacDonald's meal, and Merryn even bought him a McFlurry as an apology. They spent the afternoon sheltering from the rain under trees in the Abbey Gardens, making up life stories for their fellow shelterers. That was the sort of afternoon a teenage couple should have been enjoying, not one filled with witch-hunts.

By the time their train pulled into Stowmarket that evening, Merryn was so relaxed that she was not prepared for the dream that hit her that night.

38

This dream felt different. The watcher was not at an ethereal distance in her front row seat; she was in the middle of it. People moved around her, and she felt herself being jostled. She also felt incredibly itchy. She wanted to scratch herself through the woolly clothing, to scratch until her skin was raw but she could not move her hands. In her hair, she knew that things were alive and moving around. It was agony; she did not know which part of her body hurt more. Some of the women in this dark and smelly room were watching her in a puzzled way. How could they not be suffering as she was?

Suddenly a door opened allowing in a hint of early morning sunshine. Someone was shouting names out and women would get up and move towards the door obediently. "Anne Alderman! Jane Linstead! Sarah Spindler! Mary Abbott!" Other names were called, perhaps fifty in all, and the room began to empty. "Mary Fuller!" There was no response to this name. "Mary Fuller!"

"You can't hide in here," the voice of an old woman whispered from behind her. "Go on, Mary. Go and meet your fate; whatever that may be."

She knew then that, once again, she had become Mary Fuller in her dream. What was worse, though, was that she knew the ending to this story and she was terrified. Mary Fuller was one of the 18 hanged in Bury St Edmunds. She tried to scream herself awake, but no amount of thrashing and shouting could pull her out of the dream. "I am not Mary Fuller. I am not a witch!" she yelled in despair.

"Save it for the assizes," a man laughed as he grabbed her by the arm and pulled her so roughly out of the door that she fell on the floor. He dragged her up and pushed her towards the blinding daylight.

*Outside she had time to work out where she was before being
bundled on to one of the carts. She had just left Moyse's Hall: a
museum in her time, but a gaol in its past. She estimated that there
were at least sixty women and men divided between the two carts.
The conditions reminded her of those lorries that carried hens to
slaughterhouses.*

*"Off to the assizes with you witches," the driver sneered at
them. "And no putting curses on me, or sending your imps to get
me on the way there!" He laughed at his humour, though no one
else responded.*

*It was quiet on their journey to the assizes. A lot of them were
just relishing the fresh air, drawing in great gulps and feeling a
breeze on their skin. Those were the ones who had been there the
longest. The assizes were only held twice a year – in Lent and in
summer, so some prisoners spent many months incarcerated
there.*

*Some felt they had been lucky in surviving their imprisonment,
although they would not feel so fortunate later. Many died before
their trials, a few were pardoned, having sold their souls and
implicated their friends or relatives. Other held onto a mistaken
belief that their innocence would become obvious in front of the
judges.*

*As panic rose, she tried to plan an escape. Could she jump off
the cart and run faster than her captors? That would be simple,
but then she may well remain in this medieval town and never
return to her own body and time. Should she just stay here and re-
live Mary's fate? This was just a dream, wasn't it? Surely she
could not die. You can't die in your dreams, can you?*

Her mind was telling her to move, to run away. However, her
body was fixed to the tiny part of bench that she had found to sit
on and her head was bent down. It was as though her body
belonged to Mary Fuller, but her mind belonged to Merryn
Stearne. She was helpless. She knew that she had no choice but to
see this dream through and pray that she would survive.

*She felt tears drop silently down her cheeks and she was not
sure who they had come from - her or Mary. She wanted to weep*

for the family she may never see again, for the puppy that she had only just got to take on walks and for Jamie. Although she stoically understood the futility of her situation, she did not want to die.

The landscape was so different that she did not know where she was. She knew that they were heading towards the outskirts of Bury St Edmunds, but there were none of the modern-day markers to help. Very shortly they stopped outside a wooden gateway that was the only break in a tall, thick wall. "Where do you want this lot, Mr Fairclough?" a voice interrupted her thoughts.

"That cart can go inside," answered an official, well-dressed gentleman pointing to the cart on which she was sitting. "Take the other one to the barn with the rest."

Crowds jeered at them as their cart was taken through the gate, then to the rear of a grand building. Four other cartloads of prisoners were waiting there too: each cart containing around twenty wretches. She could not believe that all those people were to be tried that day. Surely that would not be possible.

The morning slipped slowly into the afternoon as group after group of prisoners were called into the assizes. A few of them returned with looks of abject fear on their faces. They were led back to a cart. Where the others went, she could not see.

Suddenly, she felt that the action was moving closer to her cart. "We've just got time to fit this last lot in," she heard Mr Fairclough say. "The others will have to stay in the barn. There's word the soldiers are getting closer and our men will have to travel to Cambridge soon for the battle. So there will be no one left to do these trials. Come on," he yelled at the petrified prisoners in Mary's cart. "Time for your reckoning."

The trial was something of a haze to her. The building was beautifully ornate, although many of the delicate wooden carvings were obscured behind a huge throng of on-lookers baying for blood. In the centre of the room at the back, a man dressed in violet robes sat in an exquisitely carved chair with a triangular roof above it. Wooden divides surrounded him and on either side of him were tables. In front there was a witness stand and more ornate tables holding the court officials.

Facing the judge and his officials were more gentlemen of the court, and beyond this, the prisoners were huddled at the back of a large, raised dais surrounded by iron railings. All around the prisoners were the lucky gloaters who had been allowed access to the proceedings.

Three names were called out and those prisoners stepped forwards. "There is not enough evidence to try these prisoners. You are free to leave," announced the judge. There was a mixture of cries of delight and shouts of derision as the three timid innocents pushed through the crowd to freedom.

Then the trial began in earnest. "You are all brought here in front of the court of assizes to answer to charges of witchcraft. I am Sergeant Godbold; on my right is my associate Edmund Calamy. I would like to remind the grand jury of their duty. Witchcraft is hard to prove unless the suspect has confessed, yet it is essential that these confessions are purely voluntary and unconstrained. I would draw your attention to recent confessions that have proved to be anything but voluntary and unconstrained. You must be sure that all these suspects before you have confessed willingly. The fate of their lives and immortal souls must be your primary concern."

One by one the suspects were called to answer charges. They were up there for no more than a couple of minutes, and their cases were tried and either acquitted or sentenced in that time. Very few independent witnesses were called - Matthew Hopkins and John Stearne provided most of the evidence.

As she watched, she began to get a distinct feeling that the jury and the court officials were not on the side of the witch finders. John Stearne did not help his cause however. Elizabeth Binkes of Haverhill had been sent to the assizes because, during her trial, a horsefly had buzzed around the room and landed on her, stinging her skin. That insect was said to be her imp, and a confession was signed. However, the grand jury acquitted her within one minute because she would not repeat her confession. They declared there was no evidence of witchcraft, except in the minds of the accusers. Mr Stearne was heard to condemn the judgement rather too loudly. The officials did not like such open criticism of their decision.

The prisoner standing beside Mary Fuller was a gentleman by the name of Alexander Sussums of Long Melford, near Sudbury.

He had been an acquaintance of John Stearne before the latter's work as a witch finder. Mr Sussums' mother and aunt had been hanged as witches, and his grandmother was burned at the stake. The worried man sought out his friend, John Stearne, to disclose his secret that he, too, was a witch. Mr Stearne found marks on him and committed him for the assizes. Yet, despite this confession, Sussums was sent home much to the annoyance of John Stearne.

Not all the witch finders' witches were acquitted, however. An old vicar named John Lowes was sentenced to be hanged, even though he adamantly withdrew his confession before the court. But that was not necessarily a victory for Hopkins and Stearne. After hearing about the barbaric 'swimming' torture that had proved the vicar's guilt, Sergeant Godbold ordered that, from that point forward, no more witches were to be subjected to the water ordeal.

Then it was the turn of Mary Fuller. Merryn had a feeling of being physically carried to the stand, as Mary's body took the steps but her mind took in the proceedings. As Stearne and Hopkins testified against Mary, Merryn felt detached as though she were still in the role of a watcher. Without comment, she heard the numerous stories of people falling ill after Mary had visited them, and knew there was no doubt that Mary would be found guilty. With both Alice Wright and Anne Cricke, Merryn was convinced of their innocence. With Mary Fuller, she was not so sure.

It was no surprise that five minutes later, Mary had been sentenced to death and was being led away, through a jeering crowd, past a pair of jubilant witch finders to wait in a cart for the next stage of her destiny. Only then did the reality of her position hit Merryn. She was to be hanged unless she could get out of this dream.

39

Merryn wanted to wake up but it was impossible. Her mind was awake and fighting against an unresponsive body. She was trying in vain to squeeze her eyes and force the lids up, and her limbs were ignoring her pleas to thrash themselves into consciousness.

She paused to recover energy. As her mind stopped its fight she felt her subconscious being pulled back towards sleep. Her last waking memory was a sense of desperation as she begged to stay awake.

The cart bumped over a track towards a barn. The watcher counted eighteen of them in all: sixteen women and two men. They were all silent. Whether they were thinking of final confessions before they met their Lord tomorrow or whether they were immersing themselves in memories of what they would lose, it was impossible to judge.

Very shortly, they were pushed off the cart, still shackled and still treated with contempt. The barn was divided up into sections and they were herded into a stable-like area at the very front. She thought that she could hear faint weeping and whispers from deeper within the building, but she had no desire to listen for that source. The doors were locked tight and guards stood outside.

She thought that she should be feeling something other than this numb calmness. She was going to die tomorrow. There would be no last minute pardons, no heroic rescue from the gallows, no second chances. Surely she should be panicking or crying for her lost life or angrily swearing revenge on the injustice of the witch-hunt and its protagonists. But she felt resigned. It was as though this was her fate, there was nothing she could do other than make her peace with her Lord and go to the gallows with pride.

The other condemned prisoners were similarly contemplative. Soon, they realised a fellow camaraderie and they began whispering to each other in the darkness. They found that they shared a common feeling: they wanted to go to their destiny with as much pride and dignity as such an occasion could muster. The old man, John Lowes, made a suggestion. "We must go to the gallows in silence. No confession, no begging or pleading for mercy and absolutely no penitence. There will be no reprieve for us, so let us meet our Lord with our heads held high." They all made a pact to stand firm against the accusations, and signed their agreement with a recitation of the twenty-third psalm, singing of the Lord being their shepherd.

Only one woman sat in the darkness and refused to join in. It was clear that this woman was praying for forgiveness and an escape from the noose, but Merryn knew that there would be none of that. The other prisoners curled on the floor, seeking a final night of rest though none of them slept. The pact had been made, temporary yet eternal friendships were formed; all that was left was the morning.

All too soon, Mary and her companions were dragged from the barn, blinking in the glare of the morning sunshine. That day, Wednesday 27th August 1645 had been declared a day of fasting, in which nothing was to be done except duties that were in the service of God. Hundreds of people turned out to watch the hypocritical spectacle, getting there early to get the 'best seats' at Henhowe Mound.

The condemned remained silent throughout. The woman who refused to join them, however, was not. She screamed her innocence, declared fervently to the officiating minister that she would allow Christ into her life, throwing accusations of even more vile witchcraft at her fellow prisoners.

As they hobbled off the cart, still shackled, the watcher felt more divided than ever. Through Mary's confused eyes, Merryn recognised the street she had walked down with Jamie the day before. Where Merryn expected to see houses and light industrial units, Mary saw hills and green. While Merryn was weeping inside at her impending fate, Mary held her head up in defiance as she was pushed through the braying crowd.

One by one, the 'witches' were called forward, their names and supposed crimes announced to the audience. To a backdrop of taunts and screams of horror, the prisoner's shackles were then

148

removed and they were led to the ladder that rested against the oak gallows. The 'witch' was forced to climb the ladder trembling and sometimes vomiting, then waited for the ladder to be twisted away as the noose was lowered over his or her neck.

The penitent woman who had shared her final night in the barn screeched for forgiveness right to her very end, but it was in vain. One onlooker in the crowd declared that she had found her puritanical God and should be pardoned but his words fell on deaf ears.

Soon only two were left: Mary Fuller and John Lowes. It was his turn. As he shook his hands and legs free from the loosened shackles, and walked to the ladder, he made a final request. It was granted and he was allowed to conduct his own funeral service. His final words before the ladder twisted stayed imprinted in Merryn's thoughts, "In sure and certain hope of the resurrection to eternal life. Amen."

Mary was the final victim of the day. As the shackles were removed, Merryn began to drift away into near unconsciousness. Mary was in control. The old woman felt free for the first time in many years. There was a lightness to her soul that had lain hidden under near-starvation and isolation, and she knew that she was going to a better place.

Mary walked towards the ladder and began to climb. She waited at the top and surveyed the dwindling crowd below. Seeing a familiar face, Mary locked eyes with a man and glared into the depths of his soul. She mouthed the words, "In sure and certain hope of the resurrection to eternal life". As the ladder began to twist, she smiled at him instead of finishing with 'Amen'. His heart froze and he knew that he had been cursed.

At the very moment before the ladder was turned, the Merryn inside Mary was yanked from her sleepy trance. She wanted to scream, to tear out of this woman's body, but she was powerless. Mary had gone, Merryn was going to die and there was absolutely nothing she could do about it.

Merryn saw the person that Mary cursed and she suddenly understood. The man she was looking at was her father. The Matthew Stearne of 2012 had slipped back in time to 1645 to become his long-dead relative. It was not her that the witches wanted – it was her dad.

Merryn felt Mary hiss at her as the noose tightened, "My eternal life will continue until he is destroyed. We will have revenge." Merryn's throat compressed, her breath became tighter and she slowly slipped away. The last thing she remembered was realising that her fears about Mary's true character were correct. The woman was truly a witch.

40

A scream ripped through the house at five thirty in the afternoon of 27th August 2011. Rosie ran upstairs to find her daughter lying flat on her bed, her eyes wide and manically staring at the ceiling. But she was not looking at the face; it was the neck that made Rosie clutch her mouth in horror. Stretching right around Merryn's neck was a deep, wide, red ring. The skin was cut in places and droplets of blood were appearing as the bruises coloured before her eyes. It was as though a rope had been savagely tugged against her neck.

Rosie had no idea what to do. She flinched away from touching the wound, so instead she focussed on calming her daughter's hysteria. Grasping her hand tightly, she whispered soft words of encouragement and made soothing noises. Eventually, her daughter's breathing became more even and she began to calm down. However, Merryn did not lose the look of terror in her eyes.

"What's going on?" questioned Matt as he stood panting in the doorway. He had been clearing away the last of the rubble from the shell of The Assembly Room, when he heard the horrific noise.

But as soon as he spoke, Merryn began to scream again. Her eyes widened even further and the terror in her eyes turned into to sheer dread. "Get away from me!" She screeched at her father. "You did this to us. Get away!" Merryn carried on with the same words, again and again, twisting the knife of suspicion ever deeper into her mother's mind.

"What does she mean, Matt?" Rosie said. "What did you do to her? Did you do this?"

"Don't be ridiculous!" replied the bewildered man. "How could I have done this? I was outside."

As the couple looked on, Merryn stopped screaming and started to mutter venomous words of hatred. "You did this to me. You want me dead. You want us all dead. You're a scared, evil little man. You deserve to hang, not me, not us."

When a mother is protecting her youngster, a seed of doubt easily blossoms into a tree of distrust. "Why would she say you did this if you didn't? Are you calling her a liar?" Rosie spat out the words to her husband as she bent down to hold Merryn, putting a physical barricade between father and daughter.

"I have no idea what she's going on about. I don't know why she's saying it but how can it possibly be true? I wasn't even in here. And I would never harm her, you know I wouldn't." Matt looked at his wife and realised the truth. "You don't trust me, do you? You think I would hurt my own child. How can you think that?"

Rosie could not answer, so she focussed on pacifying the whispering form on the bed. "I think you better leave, Matt. It might be for the best," she said quietly without even looking at the man she had married sixteen years ago.

The most hurtful part of the whole drama happened to Matt as he closed his daughter's bedroom door behind him. The 'Exorcist'-like mutterings stopped instantly and he heard Merryn speak to her mum. "Thank you for getting rid of that vile man. He has to pay for what he has done."

Matt knew what would happen next. Being a childhood victim of domestic violence and abuse, Rosie had always been terrified of that ugly nightmare recurring in her child's life. She clung to Merryn throughout her early childhood, refusing all offers of help. No one else was ever allowed to feed the child, let alone bath or dress her. Rosie did absolutely everything and never let Merryn out of her sight. Sometimes, Matt had been grudgingly allowed to play his part but he was always made to feel like the third member of the family.

Only when Merryn began to realise that there was life beyond her mother's apron strings did Rosie have to relinquish some of her control. At pre-school, the little girl discovered friends, and started to become a person rather than an extension of her mother.

It was hard for Rosie to let go, to trust someone else with her precious child, but with Matt's constant support and reassurance, she allowed her daughter to live a normal life.

It had hurt Matt, being on the outside of his child's babyhood. But he knew the traumas that his wife had been through, so he waited patiently to take his role as a father. His only stipulation was that Merryn remained an only child because he knew that Rosie would not cope with devoting herself to more than one. He was not sure that he could either. It had worked, though. Through her own mothering experience and her husband's non-demanding love for his family, Rosie worked through most of her demons. Until now, they were like any other family, muddling through as best they could.

Suddenly they were divided by lies. Matt slumped down on the stairs and brushed a tear from his cheek. How could Rosie believe that he would possibly harm his daughter? How could Merryn accuse him? He thought she loved him. How could he defend himself against such preposterous accusations? He knew it would take a miracle to turn the situation around.

His head in his hands, Matt started to allow all his anxiety of the past few months to flood through his mind again: everything that had happened to him since he moved here. He had thought this inheritance was a Godsend, but now it seemed like the work of the devil. He lost the job he loved and was finding it impossible to even get an interview for another. Most of their savings had gone on converting the adjoining cottage, only to find that the place was unsaleable at anything near an acceptable price. And The Assembly Room was nothing more than a decreasing pile of charred wood - useless to anyone and for anything.

Plus there were all the problems with Merryn. As if a near-brush with death was not enough, there was her new-found attitude. He had not been naïve enough to expect the teenage years to be easy, but his easy-going, likeable daughter had become obsessive, preoccupied and downright strange. At times he wondered if she was bordering on the insane. Today's behaviour was just vindictive. He had never seen that malicious streak in her before and it hurt so much.

Matt stood up and headed for the kitchen to make a cup of tea. He couldn't help wondering if he was cursed. Nothing good had happened here, and he could not shake that eerie feeling that someone or something was setting out to destroy him.

He dropped the spoon as he was stirring his tea, and it landed next to a dozing Galaxy. Usually such a gentle, bumbling dog, she leapt up in surprise. Matt leant down to retrieve the spoon and pat the dog, but it instantly pulled away. Galaxy was growling softly at him, baring her small, white, sharp teeth. Even with his limited experience of dogs, he knew she would bite him if he didn't move. So he left the spoon and backed away from her. As soon as Matt was two metres away, Galaxy shot out of the room and headed for the sanctuary of the garden. "Great," he thought. "Now even the dog hates me!"

41

They ate as a family that evening. As an apology for something he had not done, Matt prepared their favourite meal: chicken korma with garlic and coriander naan bread. Most of the food went untouched, except on Merryn's plate. After pushing the food suspiciously round her plate, she ate ravenously as if she had not eaten for weeks.

Rosie dropped the bombshell after she put the plates in the butler sink. "I think you should sleep next door tonight," she told Matt.

"Why?" asked the stunned and hurting man.

"After what happened today, Merryn and I need a bit of time and space to ourselves. I would feel safer if you were next door."

Matt couldn't help it. He lost his temper. "I haven't done anything. I haven't touched her. I wouldn't touch her. I love her. I have no idea what she thinks is going on or what she's told you, but it's all lies. Look at her! She knows it is." Matt urged Rosie to study the teenager who was sitting at the table, taking in all the fury with great relish. Rosie was oblivious to the glint in Merryn's eye and the smirk on her face.

"I'm sorry, Matt," she replied calmly. "It's my duty to protect my child, and that is the best way of doing it at the moment."

"You have nothing to protect her from. I haven't done anything to her. I am not your father!"

With that, Rosie stood up and glared at Matt. "Please go and pack a bag. I'd like you out of my house right now. Merryn's told me what you have done; the way you pinched her, how you stopped her sleeping, how you accused her of all sorts of horrific things and how you tried to drown her. And now, how you attacked her with a rope."

Matt was too horrified to speak as his muddled mind attempted to make sense of the accusations. He felt like a rabbit in headlights, knowing that his fate was well and truly sealed but having no idea how to escape. He tried to look at his wife whose eyes were downcast, so he turned to his daughter.

With a jolt, he saw that the eyes he was looking into were not those of his Merryn although they were in her face. They belonged to someone else. It was not the look of triumphant arrogance that gave them away, nor was it the mocking glint. His Merryn had beautiful green eyes to complement her dark brown hair. But these eyes were brown and slightly cloudy. He felt mesmerised as he tried to understand. No answers came, although he dredged up some long-dead memory that he had seen these eyes somewhere before.

Matt stumbled out of the room and through the front door. Oblivious to the driving rain, he slumped onto the middle of his front garden where he remained until Jamie's father rescued him many hours later and gave him refuge in their house.

Rosie stayed in the kitchen drinking tea at her wooden table and wondering how she could have been so wrong. Merryn remained beside her in silence. For a full hour, they sat there allowing the memories of that day to trace their silent echoes. Suddenly Merryn stood up. "I am going to my bed now. It has been a long and tiring day and I am very weary. Thank you for your help today, Mistress Stearne. It is only when we stick together that we will rid this world of evil. You and I will be safe now. Master Stearne has made his way in life and is paying the price." With that, Merryn fixed a puzzled Rosie with a cold stare and left the room, a whimpering Galaxy cowering away from her as she passed.

As soon as Merryn left the room, a flood of coldness swept to Rosie's very soul. She, too, had just seen what Matt saw: the eyes that did not belong. The person who had just left that room was definitely her daughter, but at the same time, she was not. It looked like her, walked like her but the eyes were all wrong and, as for the language, that was not her at all. Merryn would never talk in such a weird, formal way. Even soppy Galaxy seemed scared of her, too. Normally that puppy was in her young mistress's shadow but she had been avoiding her all day.

But if it wasn't Merryn, who was it? And how could such an inexplicable thing happen in the rational world? It must be a stressed reaction from dealing with my husband's evil behaviour, concluded Rosie. Although she did not truly believe that.

Rosie felt wearier that she had ever felt before. Just a couple of hours ago, she believed that history was repeating itself and she accepted that the only man she ever loved and trusted had betrayed her. Now that she was not so sure, she allowed reason to creep back in.

Merryn had said that her father pinched her to make a mark on her skin. Surely such a mark would have been obvious. She had also said Matt had refused to allow her to sleep for three whole days and nights. That would have meant Matt staying awake, and for a man who could and would sleep anywhere, that would never happen. As for the drowning - how could Matt have tried to drown his child in a garden pond without anyone noticing?

Rosie went up to Merryn's door and knocked. Without waiting for an answer, she went in. "Show me your neck," she demanded of the figure sitting upright on the bed, looking out of the window at the pond in the garden.

"Why would you want to see my neck, mistress?" it demanded. Rosie was starting to sweat with fear, despite the chill in the room. It was not even pretending to be Merryn. The eyes that were trying to hold her in their glare were cruel, and the voice carried more than a faint hint of an old-fashioned accent that complemented the dialect.

"I want to make sure it's healing up okay," Rosie stammered.

"What is it you mean, mistress?" the voice taunted. "My neck is in perfectly fine health. Why don't you take a look?"

With trembling hands, Rosie took hold of the end of the triangular bandage she had dressed Merryn's neck with earlier. She started to pull it away gently, not wanting to damage any newly scabbing skin. She was also desperately trying to avoid touching this creature.

"Are you scared of hurting me Mistress?" the non-Merryn taunted.

Rosie ignored it and kept pulling the bandage away. There was absolutely no resistance and in seconds, Rosie saw why. There was no mark on the creature's neck. All the grazes, bruises, cuts and blood that covered Merryn's neck earlier had vanished. It was as if Rosie had imagined everything.

The creature started laughing in delight as it looked at Rosie's ashen face.

"Who are you?" whispered Rosie.

"I am your daughter, of course, Mistress Stearne. I am the child who will look after you and help you in times when the man of the house is away fighting the troubles. Or fighting witches, which is the path your husband has chosen to take. He is suffering for that, Mistress Stearne, and he will suffer more until he has paid his dues."

"Where's Merryn?"

"Merryn is dead, Mistress Stearne. She died on the gallows because she was a witch, and your husband sent her there. I am Merryn now, and I will be with you forever."

Rosie was frantic. Never had superstition been allowed a glimpse into her life, harsh reality being the criteria on which she based her decisions. Now she was faced with a creature that claimed it was something that could not exist, that was babbling away about witches and hangings. This could not be happening. She must be having a nightmare or someone must be playing the sickest joke in history.

"You don't believe me, do you, Rosemary Stearne. Do you want me to show you?" The creature was enjoying herself. "Go and lie down, Rosemary. You are sleepy. Don't you feel really tired? So tired that you could sleep for a week, a month, a lifetime? Go to bed, Rosie-Posie."

Moving as though in a trance, Rosie left the room and went into her bedroom where she lay down on her bed. She was asleep the second she shut her eyes, and then she was dreaming.

42

Merryn thought that she was awake for a split-second, until she realised the terrible truth. She was still in her dream, trapped in the nightmare of August 1645. The only difference being that now she was the only spirit possessing Mary Fuller's body. In her previous dream, she felt a battle between the two spirits. She had been seeing through the eyes of Mary, but she had not become that woman. Now she was Merryn in her mind but Mary in her body. And she was standing on a falling ladder with a noose around her neck, about to be hanged as a witch.

Time slowed down as she saw a horrific sight right before her. Finally recognisable in his smart, expensive clothing, sporting a large, fanciful hat and beard was her father. He was the man she had come to know as John Stearne. He was smiling and accepting nods of congratulation from the spectator beside him. Merryn silently begged him to look at her, to realise that he was about to murder his own daughter.

However, standing right next to him was Merryn herself. Except it was not Merryn; it was her body, but not her mind and those brown eyes were most definitely not hers. Mary Fuller was in her body and from that smug smile directed straight at Merryn, she was perfectly happy there.

Suddenly there was a movement through the crowd. It was an amazing sight. The surrounding action was still taking place in the slow motion that only movies and dreams can produce; yet a woman was pushing through to the front of the crowd in real time. They reacted and pushed back but at less than a quarter of her speed. Only three other people were in that woman's time warp: Merryn, her father and Mary.

The woman shoved to the foot of the gallows shouting. "You've got the wrong one! That's not her! That's my daughter." Then through the dirt on the woman's face, the blackened gaps where her teeth had been, the scruffy, uncombed hair sprouting out from underneath a worn bonnet, Merryn locked eyes with the newcomer. As the woman fainted, Merryn recognised her mother.

So, too, did Mary Fuller and Merryn's father. The look of panic and bewilderment lasted only a matter of seconds on Matt's face. He was starting to stutter out a demand for an explanation when something more horrific began to happen. Right before their disbelieving eyes, his features began to smudge and fade. It was as though someone had taken a giant rubber and was erasing sections of him. The strong jaw-line and cheekbones remained, but the gap between his nose and lips was made narrower. His eyes were moved slightly further apart, and they changed from their usual green colour to a dark, cold brown. His eyebrows were rubbed away, and made thinner. There was a definite family resemblance between Matt and this new man, but they were not the same person.

By now, time on the outside of this action had frozen into a tableau, as though these four characters were leading players and the crowd their supporting chorus. The person that had been Matt turned to his companion, the shell of Merryn's body. "Mary Fuller, I sentenced you to death for crimes of witchcraft. Do you wish to appeal against the sentence?" This was said in a mocking tone; the man smiling sardonically as he spoke.

"Mary Fuller is about to hang on the gallows for her crimes against our God-fearing society, Master Stearne," Mary replied, challenging the man to prove her wrong.

John Stearne glanced briefly up at the shell of Mary's body, still balanced on a ladder with a noose nestled around her neck. "That is not Mary Fuller," he stated. "What act of witchcraft have you committed now to cause that poor wretch to lend you her body? Or do you think I will hang a person without first trying them? Do you believe that I am so totally lawless in my pursuit of a pure society?"

"Yes, Master Stearne, I do," smiled Mary. "Hang her. Who will know?"

Rosie was starting to stir from her slumped position on the ground at the foot of the ladder. She thought that she was awake when she first found herself running up that hill and towards the throng of people. But everything had been alien to her: the combined smells of garlic, ale and strong body-odour, the uncomfortable heaviness of her clothing and the taste of decay in *her mouth. It was somewhere so far from her own life that she knew she must be dreaming. It felt so real though.*

The sight of the gallows with the long row of bodies swinging from them made Rosie want to be sick there and then, but she knew she had to hold it together, to see if the creature was right about Merryn. With horror, she realised that it was true.

It was the eyes. The body about to be sent to its death was that of an old woman, with a shock of white, messy hair, and skin sagging around her face and neck. But the eyes belonged to a young girl, and Rosie saw immediately that they belonged to her daughter. Perhaps there was another connection too; that impenetrable mother/daughter bond that most fortunate parents share. Whatever it was, Rosie knew instantly that her Merryn's mind and soul were about to be destroyed forever.

Then she saw Matt, dressed up as though he were some sort of country squire. He was smugly receiving praise for the act that was about to happen. He would be responsible for the death of his only child and he was proud of it. Suddenly, Rosie felt a strength rise up inside her. She was in control again, and was not about to let this creature destroy her family.

"Let my daughter go," Rosie said calmly to the person in Merryn's body.

Mary laughed an evil, penetrating cackle. "I am your daughter, Rosemary. Look at me. I look like her, do I not?"

"You are not Merryn. I don't know or even care who you are. Just let her go."

John Stearne turned to Rosie and smiled the smile of pure evil. "Do tell me who you are, dear lady, and who that body there belongs to."

"That body belongs to my daughter Merryn, and that thing there cannot have it. As for me, I am Rosie Stearne and I want my child back." Her newly rediscovered strength was deserting her and she knew that she was about to cry.

The witch hunter studied her. "Are you related to me, by any chance, you and that child?"

"How can I be related to you? I don't know you. I don't know where I am, when this is, or even what is going on. I just want my daughter back safely at home with me."

"And where is home?" he continued softly.

"Hitcham in Suffolk," she began to lose the battle against the tears. "Please get her down."

"I remember Hitcham well," he sighed. "A successful place, I believe. A God-believing town of puritanical faith. And Stowmarket I hear is more cleansed too thanks to my efforts. Mary Fuller, I demand that you retake your place in history. It is an act of witchcraft to alter the course of time to suit your own needs. It is also an act of witchcraft to possess another soul. Do you wish to confess to being a witch? Do you wish to renege on the pact you made with your fellow prisoners and confess?"

He locked eyes with the creature, which seemed to shrink under his stare. Then she jutted out her chin, straightened her shoulders and spoke with a defiance that she did not feel. "I will not give you the satisfaction of a confession. Whatever I am is my business, no one else's. I will not be known as one of your triumphs. I will not give you that satisfaction."

John Stearne was watching her discomfort with great delight, knowing he had cornered her, yet admiring her pride. He felt troubled, however. He could not understand what was happening. He was awake, yet he was not awake. There was a strange woman and her daughter here, who seemed to be related to him, yet they were obviously not of this time. Witchcraft was most definitely at work here; this was the truest form of it he had ever witnessed, and he did not like it.

With astonishing dignity, Mary Fuller walked for the final time in Merryn's body towards the ladder leading up to the scaffold of the gallows. She climbed slowly but calmly, accepting that the fight was lost yet preparing herself for the next stage in her journey. It was as though she had absolutely no fear of her impending death.

It all happened so suddenly. Mary reached the top of the ladder and seemed to step into her former body. At that moment, Merryn vanished as did her mother, and the frozen tableau sprang to life, jeering and cheering. As the hangman continued to twist the ladder away, she mouthed the words, "In sure and certain hope of resurrection to eternal life, I will ruin you, John Stearne" to the witch finder standing before her. Her final 'Amen' broke off in between the two syllables as she fell.

43

The following morning, Matt walked downstairs in the Foster house. After being rescued from the front garden the previous evening, he spent hours off-loading all his problems on Nick. His tales of woe and bad luck grew as the whiskey flowed. By two in the morning, both Matt and Nick were convinced that someone was out to ruin him. The invisible culprit had not only destroyed his career, thus breaking him financially, but had also thrown a huge wedge in his family happiness through Merryn's accusations.

At first, Nick did not know what to think. His wife, Jane, was a social worker and she grudgingly admitted that Merryn's behaviour would set most alarm bells ringing. The girl was clearly disturbed in many ways. That incident with the pond was bizarre, and all her health problems – the sleep deprivation, the night terrors, the strange self-harming – were indications of an inner turmoil. Something did not feel right to Jane, however. She knew better than to believe in the illusion of the outwardly happy family image, but the Stearnes were just that.

Jane wondered whether it was just a case of Merryn being slightly unstable, and her parents suffering as a result. She liked Merryn and saw how happy she made her son. A lot of Jamie's seriousness had smoothed away since the pair became a couple and he was now a lot more interested in having fun. Coping with Merryn's problems had also showed a remarkably sensitive, caring side to his personality. But she hoped that the teenage romance would fizzle away; she wasn't sure that coping with a girlfriend with mental health issues was fair on a young man.

In Nick's opinion, the Stearnes were just a normal family who had been thrown a whole heap of bad luck recently. In a sober state, however, he drew the line at agreeing with Matt that there was some supernatural influence involved. Perhaps it helped Matt to cope; not a particularly helpful coping strategy though.

He must admit that he had been more concerned than his wife when Matt told him about Merryn's accusations. Nick conceded that there was no possible way Matt could have harmed his daughter, but why had she named him as her assailant? She was not a vindictive child, and she appeared to have a close relationship with her father. So why would she suddenly turn against him? Once he saw Matt safely tucked up in their spare bedroom that night, Nick made sure he checked that Jamie's door was firmly shut. It was probably lies, but he would take no chances with his son's safety.

Matt looked far from rested when he greeted Nick the following morning. He accepted the coffee gratefully and sat in the large armchair beside the window, looking out at his own house. "How are you feeling?" asked Nick.

"Bit of a headache," Matt confessed. "I think I owe you a bottle of whiskey. Sorry. I'll replace it."

Nick brushed away his offer. "You didn't sleep too well. I heard you shout out a couple of times."

"I had a really weird nightmare. It was so realistic that I felt like I was there. You'd think I was totally mad if I told you what it was about."

"Try me," Nick offered. He could see that Matt was embarrassed but he thought it might help him to offload. There might be some sort of clue in there too.

"Okay, but don't call the men in white coats. It was like I was back in time – I don't know how many hundreds of years – and I was standing at the front of a huge crowd of people. I was dressed up like a country squire or something with a big black hat and a beard. It was horrible," he shuddered. "I was watching people being hanged. There were loads of them; I don't know how many, at least fifteen. And the worst thing was that I was really pleased. I kept getting congratulated, being told that I'd done a great job to society and God. I even saw an old man being hung. He must've been at least eighty. Then it all got even weirder.

"There was a woman on the gallows and she was about to be hanged. The noose was round her neck and the executioner was about to kick the ladder away. Then she looked at me. She just stared at me and … this is stupid, I know... I felt like she was cursing me. But then her eyes changed and they became Merryn's eyes."

"How do you know it was you?" asked Nick, not knowing how to react to this bizarre story.

"They kept calling me 'Master Stearne'. It was like I was some kind of hero," Matt finished off his coffee and started up the story again.

"That wasn't all though. I remember waking up, but I must've gone back to sleep because I had another dream."

"You definitely had too much to drink," joked Nick feeling disturbed by all this. He was glad that Jane was out with the dog, as he would hate to see her reaction. She would have been on the phone, calling in social services reinforcements.

"Maybe," Matt grinned ruefully. "The second dream was the same in that I was in that odd outfit again, in the same crowd. It was like someone had rewound the dream to the final hanging. Everything was the same. I had to watch the poor old man hang again, then the final one climbed the ladder. It was the same old woman with Merryn's eyes and she was pleading to be saved. I've got some vague memory of Rosie being in it."

Nick put a fresh cup of coffee in front of his friend and neighbour. He did not know what to say. He was sure that there was some psychological explanation for the dreams. Whatever they meant, though, was a mystery to him; a mystery he did not want to know the answer to.

"Thanks for putting up with me," Matt interrupted his troubled thoughts. "You must think I'm a total lunatic. I'll go and see Rosie and Merryn in a minute and see if we can work things out."

"And if you can't?" Nick dared to ask.

Matt looked at him with defeat written all over his face. "I don't know what I'll do. They're my life; they're all I've got left. I've got no job, no money, an inheritance that is a millstone, and a family who think I am a child-beater or even a paedophile. If they don't want me, I don't know what I'll do."

44

Jamie had been listening in at the doorway throughout this whole conversation. He had also tried to glean information from the adults' drunken ramblings of the previous night. It was only two days since their trip to Bury St Edmunds but it felt like a lifetime. He had not seen Merryn, but he pieced together something of the story. He would not believe that Matt could attack his own daughter and he realised that somehow, she must have experienced a witch's hanging.

He wanted to go in the lounge and tell Matt that he believed him, tell both of them about everything that had been going on: the haunting, the dreams. But how could he? It sounded ridiculous even to someone like himself who had come to believe in it. Instead he left the men to their coffee and went to Merryn's house.

Jamie's first thought as he ran across the greensward between the houses was how awful the weather was. It was raining torrentially, and the dark purply grey clouds were threatening a tremendous storm. Rosie was unusually quiet when she opened the door. Instead of chatting to him, she left him standing in the hallway as she called Merryn.

His girlfriend trailed down the stairs five minutes later, wrapped in a fluffy pink dressing gown and wiping sleep from her eyes. She said nothing, just went to Jamie and put her arms around him. "Do you want to tell me about it?" he asked when she finally loosened her grip.

Half an hour later, they were sitting on the sofa in the lounge and Jamie heard the whole tale; how Merryn had dreamed that she was Mary Fuller, how she was nearly hanged, how she saw both her parents in her dream, how Mary tried to escape her fate by possessing Merryn, how John Stearne had corrected the course of history by offering Mary the choice of confession or dispossession, how her mother believed the accusations against her father.

"My mum was there. She saw Mary in my body. She was tricked into believing that Mary was me. She saw me nearly hang. But she won't talk about it. She thinks there's a logical explanation. She's been on the phone to the Calor gas people already cos she thinks we had a gas leak and it affected our brains. I can't make her see."

"Do you know what you - okay, not you, but Mary when she looked liked you – told her about your dad?" asked Jamie.

"Not really, but I've got a pretty good idea. She keeps asking me if Dad really hurt me, and if he's ever done it before. I keep telling her over and over again that Dad would never hurt me. She won't listen though. She keeps saying that I don't have to cover up for him and that I should be open and honest about it, not be scared of the consequences. It's like she's tried and convicted him without even giving the evidence a chance."

Rosie chose that moment to poke her head around the door and ask the couple if they wanted some tea. She knew that they would both decline, but she needed to check up on them. This half hour gap was the longest Rosie had left Merryn alone since the previous night's incident, even to the point that she had slept on the small floor area in her daughter's bedroom.

Although 'slept' was probably the wrong word. She had woken from that horrendous dream and immediately ran to her daughter's side to find her fast asleep, yet moaning softly with tears streaming down her cheeks. Rosie could not bring herself to touch her child, fearful that it was the other creature again. But she could not leave her either, the need for maternal protection stronger than it ever had been.

Rosie kept replaying the frighteningly realistic images from the dream. She truly felt like it actually happened, but that could not be possible. And surely the terrible creature that was here yesterday was part of the same dream. She could explain that one, however, much more easily. Seeing her only child hurt so cruelly as that had brought back all the suppressed memories of her own childhood, and so a nightmare became a reality. There had been no creature, no hangings; and the only potential threat to her daughter came from her own family.

Logical explanations, therefore, helped her cope. Rosie was also an expert at forgetting what she could not handle; she had a lot of experience. Dealing with her daughter's allegations was not so easy. In her heart, she could not believe that Matt would harm Merryn; they shared such a strong bond and always seemed so happy together. But the evidence showed otherwise. As with all Rosie's major life decisions, her head won the battle.

When Matt knocked at the door an hour later, Rosie's downcast eyes gave him all the answers he needed. Without speaking, he went upstairs and packed a small bag. He went into the lounge to see Merryn before he left. It annoyed him immensely that his wife insisted on standing in the doorway watching his every move.

"Dad. You're not going are you?" Merryn panicked as soon as Matt came to her. He put Galaxy on the floor so that he could sit next to his daughter.

"Just for a little while, love. Just till things calm down a bit." He tried to keep the tears from his eyes but they were there in his voice.

"You can't go," she yelled back. "You haven't done anything. Please don't go."

Matt could not hold back the tears as he held his daughter and let her cry in his arms. "It's not for long, love. I'll be home soon, I promise."

"Where will you go, Dad?"

"Do you remember Ray who I used to work with? The one in Colchester with a daughter your age? We went to their house for a barbecue about a year ago."

"You can't stand his wife, Dad," wailed Merryn. "You can't go there."

"She's not too bad," Matt smiled. "Just a bit stuck up. Anyway, I'm not going to their house. He said I could stay in their caravan in Felixstowe until I get sorted. I won't be too far from you, and I'll get a nice bit of sea-air while I'm at it."

"Can I come, Dad?"

"No," interrupted Rosie. "You're back at school in a few days and I haven't organised your uniform yet."

"You mean you won't let me," Merryn spat back. "Because you reckon my dad will hurt me or something."

"That's enough, Merryn," said Matt soothingly. "I'll be getting off now. We all just need a bit of calming down time. Things have been pretty bad recently. I'll see you soon."

As soon as Matt pulled the front door shut, Merryn ran to her room yelling at Jamie to stay there because she was getting changed and going to his house. In record time, she was back downstairs, heading for Jamie's house with her boyfriend and puppy running behind her and ignoring her mother's shouts to get back home immediately.

Jamie, Merryn and Galaxy went in through the kitchen door and heard the Fosters talking about Matt. "I did offer, but he didn't want to stay here," Nick said. "He couldn't bear to be so close to Merryn and not be able to see her. You don't think he really did anything to her, do you?"

"In my social worker opinion, all the evidence suggests something odd is happening over there. But my gut reaction is no," his wife replied.

"He truly believes that someone is out to get him, you know. I feel really sorry for him. There must be some way of helping him."

Galaxy chose that moment to dash into the lounge and drop a toy at Nick's feet. "Hello there," he said. "How long have you been there?"

Jamie had reopened the back door silently and now slammed it shut so his parents didn't suspect. Merryn was subjected to well-meaning but painful questions regarding how she was feeling before she could escape to the sanctuary of Jamie's room.

"Tell me again what you saw in your dream," Jamie insisted once they were alone.

"What, all of it?"

"No, just the bit about your dad."

So Merryn repeated how her father had been there, revelling in the executions, but how he had changed into another person.

"I have a theory," Jamie stated slowly when she had finished. "It may all be rubbish but bear with me. In your dream, your dad was John Stearne, right?"

Merryn nodded, and he continued. "And your dad is a direct descendant of John Stearne right?" Another nod. "These witches you keep seeing were all tried and died because of John Stearne right?" Merryn had started to get a glimpse of where this was going. "What did you say Mary Fuller's final words were? Something about resurrection to eternal life and I will ruin you? Am I right?" This time the nods were met with a smile of sorts.

"To sum up, you are being haunted because those witches want to send a message to your dad. They want to ruin him by hurting the most precious thing he's got – his daughter."

"That's brilliant," yelled Merryn giving her boyfriend a huge kiss on the cheek and making him blush furiously. "Right then, genius. What can we do about it?"

His smile dropped. "I don't know."

45

"Did you know that Matthew Hopkins only lived for two years after he killed all those witches in Bury St Edmunds?" Jamie commented to Merryn the following morning.

Once again, they were in his bedroom. Merryn could not face being at home without her father there, putting up with seeing her mother traipsing around the place like a lost soul. They had not spoken since Matt left yesterday.

"I thought he was hung like the witches," Merryn replied.

"That is what a lot of people think. But it might have been less spectacular than that. Apparently, he got tuberculosis and died in his home at Manningtree. He'd wasted away to nothing and must have really suffered at the end."

"Good!" was Merryn's vehement reply. "What about John Stearne? What happened to him?"

"The witches got their way. He died a ruined man. Apparently, he was running low on money when he returned to his home town of Lawshall, near Bury St Edmunds. He said it was because some of the places he cleansed had not paid him. He lost even more money in a court case in 1654, and started calling himself a 'yeoman' and not a 'gentleman'. That's like going from a posh person to a commoner. His neighbours hated him and his son, John, died young. John senior died in 1671."

"Good again!" Merryn announced, then her expression changed. "What I don't understand, though, is why they want to destroy my dad when they've already destroyed John Stearne."

"Maybe they don't know," reasoned Jamie. "They all died when he was at the peak of his success."

"If they can haunt me so easily, surely they could've seen into his life and got some sort of revenge that way. Would've saved me a heck of a lot of hassle."

"You're asking me to come up with a logical explanation to something that is totally illogical, Merryn. I don't know. Maybe you're more sensitive. Maybe you moving to your place with your family links triggered something. Maybe ghosts don't do logical thought like us mortals, us intelligent ones anyway."

"It's not funny," Merryn attacked Jamie with his pillow until he apologised. "What can I do to show them that he did end up destroyed and that now they can leave my dad alone?"

For hours they discussed ideas but came up empty-handed. The only connection Merryn had with John Stearne's victims was through her dreams, and they came to her then; she never sought them. Séances and ouija boards were for horror movies, so they were discounted with another pillow attack.

Eventually, an invitation from Nick to visit Matt at the caravan broke the planning. It was instantly accepted and all talk of conjuring up accused witches was put on hold. Merryn and Jamie laughed as they fought to bundle Galaxy into the boot of the car. The puppy sensed the excitement and was not happy with being confined when she felt she should be playing.

Rosie watched as they drove away, her heart in her throat. She wished so much that she was in the car with them, seeing the person that she loved. She wanted to run after them and shout, "Tell Matt to come home. Tell him I forgive him!" But she knew that she did not have to find forgiveness; she had to find belief.

It must have been the sea air that made Merryn sleep so deeply that night. In fact, she slept like the proverbial baby for the next five nights. They returned to school on a Thursday, but Merryn's excitement at seeing her friends again was dampened by her domestic upset. Her father was still in the caravan and her mother was now so depressed that she had sat on the sofa for the whole of the previous day watching rubbish on television.

Merryn returned home from school that day with a bubble of optimism that soon popped as she walked through the door. Her mum was sitting at the kitchen table holding a tissue, red-eyed and weeping silently.

"What's happened?"

"It's your dad. He's been offered a job."

"That's good, isn't it?" Merryn was confused.

"It's in China. He's been head-hunted by some global company. They're offering him a massive salary, a luxury apartment and maids to do all his housework. It's such a brilliant opportunity." Rosie reached for another tissue.

Merryn felt stunned. If her dad were in China, she would never get to see him. Their money worries might be over, but so would their family. "He doesn't have to take it, Mum. If you asked him to come home, he would. You know he'd rather have us than some fancy job thousands of miles away."

Rosie said nothing, so Merryn started looking for a distraction. On the table by her elbow was a pile of post that had been left unopened. Merryn flicked through it, discounting it all until she reached an envelope addressed to her father and bearing a National Lottery logo on the front. Without asking for permission, she opened it, hoping that it would be notification of a massive win. It wasn't.

It was to do with money, though. "Mum, do you remember that, ages ago, Dad applied for lottery funding to renovate The Assembly Room? Then it all got stopped because of the weather, and the grant was put on hold."

"Vaguely," muttered Rosie.

"They've re-granted it but for double the amount. Provided he can submit all sorts of stuff that they want – plans, budgets and all that – it's all ours. Can I call Dad and tell him?"

Without waiting for a response, Merryn ran to the phone and called Matt. This time, she did not care about the cost of a call from a landline to a mobile. She did not get the reaction she wanted, however.

Merryn had hoped that Matt would be so excited that he would pack his bag and come straight home to get started on the paperwork. He hesitated, however.

"It's good news, Merryn. But I'll be too busy with this new job," he said with absolutely no enthusiasm in his voice at all. "It's a fabulous job, you know. Something I've always wanted to do. Brilliant opportunities."

There was so much resignation in Matt's voice that Merryn lost her temper. "Why can't you stop being so stubborn and just come home?"

"It's not up to me. I can't come home at the moment. You know why I can't, Merryn. Besides, China would be a great place to visit. I get a free plane ticket for relatives once a year, so you'll be able to come and see me."

That did not help Merryn's anger. "Will you and Mum just talk to each other? If you go to China, then they've won. They've ruined you. Do you think you'll be happy? You won't. Don't phone me again until you've decided to come home."

Merryn hung up and curled up on her bed, feeling guilty for hurting her dad but knowing that she had been given no choice. The last thought in her mind before she fell asleep was that, for the first time ever, she wanted to see a ghost.

46

The following day, Merryn was deep in conversation with Jamie as the bus pulled up in front of their houses after a long and boring day at school. They were discussing Ed's latest dumped girlfriend. This one had reacted particularly badly; possibly because he chose to do the deed by changing his Facebook status to 'Free and Single again! Sorry, Jo!'

So they did not notice the car at the side of Merryn's house until they stepped off the bus. "Dad's home!" she screamed running towards her front door and forgetting to give Jamie his customary farewell kiss. She dashed into the house, even ignoring the puppy manically trying to get her attention.

Matt was sitting at the kitchen table drinking tea, but he was quick to jump up and be cuddled by his daughter. For a few long minutes, they stood together, then Merryn pulled away. "Is this a visit, Dad?" she whispered.

There was silence for a moment as the adults looked at each other. It was Rosie who answered. "I hope not. I've been stupid and I hope that your dad will forgive me and come home for good." Matt didn't answer; he just crossed to his wife and held her instead.

Earlier that morning, Rosie had phoned Matt that morning and asked if they could talk. It had all been too much for her. Loneliness and time for rational thought made her realise that all the accusations thrown at Matt had no grounding. And she missed him; more than she thought possible. So she swallowed her pride and phoned. Matt got to the house in record time.

"What about China?" asked Merryn.

"I've turned it down," her dad replied. "I don't want to be that far away from my family. Something will come up, and until it does, I'll have you two to annoy every day."

They spent a happy evening together, taking a drive to Felixstowe to collect Matt's belongings. Galaxy went along and they walked along the sea front eating chips and watching the puppy run away from the seagulls. There was no indication of the nightmare that would follow their idyllic reunion.

The dream Merryn had been hoping for came that night. She had no idea where she was; it was one of those strange dreams that seem to exist in a vacuum. Then images started materialising before her eyes.

She became aware that she was standing in a field of tall grass. A tall, natural hedgerow surrounded it, and it was totally empty. A large bonfire suddenly appeared in the dead centre of the field. Something was upright in the middle of the bonfire, standing in a wooden barrel, but she could not make out what it was. As she squinted to get a better look at the object, she noticed small swirls of smoke coming from the base of the bonfire. The smoke became denser and flames started to crackle from the dry wood. Merryn watched, mesmerised.

To her amazement, three figures emerged from the flames. They were willowy, wispy clouds of air that took on human features as they stood away from the fire. Merryn recognised them immediately as Alice Wright, Anne Cricke and Mary Fuller.

"Mistress Stearne, I am pleased to meet you again," Mary sneered. "I feel like I know you so well."

Merryn noticed that while Mary seemed to be taking the lead, Alice Wright was hiding in the background as much as she could. "I wanted to talk to you," Merryn said hoping that her fear would not be too obvious.

"We are aware of that but we had no need of you," commented Mary. "It had worked. The Stearne descendant was ruined, so you were no longer necessary. You thought it was all about you, did you not? Oh, the arrogance of the young, ladies; they believe that the world was made for them." She looked to her companions who nodded obediently.

"We had to show you what he did. You had to believe, you had to suffer in order for him to suffer. He would never have believed us, but you, with your youthful gullibility, wanted the excitement

of a haunting. He murdered these ladies, and myself, in the name of religion and a pure society, then he stole their homes. He humiliated us, tortured us and hurt us. He ruined the evening days of our lives, so his life had to be destroyed."

"He was destroyed," interrupted Merryn. "John Stearne died a broken man. He was hated by his neighbours, he was spending more money than he had, his son was dead."

The women laughed scornfully. "Do you think we are not aware of that?" derided Anne. "We watched his demise, we danced at his funeral – not just us, the others too; those who had not made their peace with their Lord."

Merryn could feel the heat from the rising flames as Mary bent down to hiss in her face. "That, however, Mistress Stearne is not enough. Who knows how many of us innocents he murdered – him and his friend, Master Hopkins? The Stearnes must be made to pay, and we have done our duty. Your great uncle, John Stearne. Do you know of his sad demise into madness? Look into your family history, Mistress Stearne. Is there not a lot of ill luck amongst the Stearne menfolk?"

Family history had never been a topic of conversation at the dinner table. Merryn realised that the past was a taboo subject for her mother, and her father's side of the family had always been very sparse. There were never any large family gatherings such as weddings, christenings or funerals.

"Your own father had to suffer too, and we nearly succeeded. No job, no reputation, no home and no family – a ruined man," Anne stated.

"But he resisted," said Mary with fury in her voice. "He took back his place in his family and his home as though he has nothing to feel guilty of. He must suffer."

"My father hasn't done anything!" yelled Merryn in desperation.

"Your father is from John Stearne's line," was Mary's reply. The old woman turned slowly to face the fire, a cruel smile glinting on her face. Her companions copied her, although the elation was not apparent on Alice Wright's face. Even Anne Cricke's jubilant smile looked forced. Merryn followed their stares and realised with horror that she could see clearly the figure in the centre of the fire. It was her father!

"Dad!" Merryn screamed as she threw back the covers on her bed. "Dad!" She began coughing and noticed that smoke was creeping through the gap under her closed door. Merryn reached for the glass of water on her bedside table and threw it over a tee shirt that was lying on the floor. Holding the wet cloth over her face, she pushed open her bedroom door.

"Dad! Mum!" she screamed again. There were flames licking at the door leading to their bedroom. She tried to get closer, but the fire was too fierce. Instead, she ran down the stairs to phone 999, Galaxy close by her heels.

After a frantic phone call, Merryn attempted to get back upstairs to her parents. It was impossible, however, to get through the wall of flames and smoke blocking the stairs. "Merryn!" a woman's voice yelled. "Get out now!"

Rosie was standing at the front door, holding a writhing, terrified white cat. "The fire brigade are on their way. Get out!"

Merryn coughed and stumbled her way towards her mother and out into the night air. Mother, daughter, cat and puppy sat on the front garden watching helplessly as flames lit up the front bedroom windows. "Is Dad still in there?" she asked. Her mother did not answer; her tears gave the reply.

Rosie had been woken up before the fire started by the sound of cats fighting. Knowing that Snowdrop could be a bully, she went downstairs to intervene. After fruitlessly following caterwauling for ten minutes, she found Snowdrop asleep under a bush outside the shell of The Assembly Room. Oblivious to the drama within, Rosie was about to return indoors when she saw her daughter amongst the flames.

Most of the neighbours were either outside or staring from behind windows as the fire engines arrived. The Fosters were with Merryn and her mum, trying to convince them to come inside and wait in their house. For two and a half long hours, they drank tea, paced the room and stared out of the window. Despair was mounting and as each minute ticked by without Matt reappearing, their hopes for him faded. At one point, they heard an ambulance scream up to the house, but they did not hear it leave.

At around three o'clock in the morning, there was a knock at the Foster's front door. There stood a very sooty, weary fire fighter, wearing a look of shock and bemusement on his face.

178

Immediately, Rose and Merryn jumped up demanding to know Matt's fate.

"It's a miracle," he sighed. "Mr Stearne is okay." Once the cheers died down, the man continued. "We found him hiding in the chimney breast that runs in the middle of both the houses. He said that he woke up and found his bed on fire. The flames were blocking the door and the window. Apparently, he guessed that there was a sort of alcove within the chimney breast because he'd found one in the house next door. He said something about finding some strange things in there recently. Also, he reckoned that he would get some air from the chimney. It was his only hope."

"Has he been there all this time?" asked Rosie.

"Yes; right from when the fire first started. But he hasn't been awake all the time. He must have passed out at some point, maybe due to smoke inhalation. He was asleep when we found him. Don't worry, though, he is fine. The paramedics are trying to persuade him to go to hospital at the moment to be checked over, but he is adamant that he is okay. So they've allowed him to stay here provided they have a look at him, which they're doing now."

"I can't thank you enough," Rosie sobbed quietly. "You saved my husband."

"It wasn't me," the fire fighter replied modestly. "I reckon he must have had some sort of guardian angel looking out for him tonight. He must be the luckiest man alive. No way he should've survived that inferno. I wish I could say your house had been gifted too, but I'm afraid I can't. It's always the same with these thatched places."

The group followed the fire fighter outside and looked in disbelief at what was left of the house. Other than a huge, brick chimney breast standing erect in the ground, there was nothing but ashes and charcoaled debris.

47

True to his word, Matt refused any offer of hospitalisation. He was not injured although his throat was sore and his head ached. But he had only vague memories of the fire. Later that morning, after his family had taken advantage of the hospitality of the Fosters, he talked of what he could remember.

"The first thing I knew was when I woke up and it looked like the bed was on fire. It was weird, though. It started on the edges like a ring. I managed to jump out of the centre of the flames and I remembered the alcove in next-door's chimney breast, so I went in there. I don't really remember anything else until I felt someone pushing my arm and calling my name. I must've fallen asleep, I suppose.

"I think I had a sort of dream when I was asleep, although it may have been the effect of the smoke. I heard voices but I couldn't see pictures. I sound like I've gone mad, don't I? Blame it on the smoke! Seriously, I heard some women shouting about burning the witch, then a man shouted, "We do not burn witches in England." Then he whispered something to me, but I can't remember what it was. Something to do with blood ties."

While Nick, Jane and Rosie teased Matt about how much of his brain had been fogged up by the smoke, Merryn and Jamie looked at each other.

Earlier that morning, she had told him about her dream and the resulting fire. "I reckon that John Stearne must've been protecting Dad," she whispered.

"Certainly sounds like it," agreed Jamie. "Do you think it's over now? They can't do anything else, can they?"

"You know, I think it is," Merryn smiled. "Raising a fire like that is surely an act of witchcraft. Weren't witches often accused because they set out to harm others? Isn't that what they were trying to do to my dad?"

Jamie put on a confused face. "Does that mean that they were witches all along? They weren't these innocent victims that everyone believes they were. You're not going to tell me that John Stearne and Matthew Hopkins were right are you?"

"Absolutely not! And I'm not saying they were witches; not while they were alive at any rate. Mind you, I have real doubts about Mary Fuller – she seemed to have some weird powers. Still, I think they chose to use witchcraft when they were dead as a way of getting revenge cos they had no power when they were alive. Trouble is that using magic like that would've been seen as witchcraft and they'd always refused to confess. So, if they'd let Dad die, that would be like admitting they were witches all along."

"And," continued Jamie, "John Stearne saw them using witchcraft to destroy your dad and they didn't want him to have the satisfaction of being right so they stopped. Therefore, John Stearne saved your dad."

"I don't think I'll tell Dad that," laughed Merryn. "I'm not sure how he'd feel about having a ghost as a guardian angel."

"Especially not a witch-hunting murderer of a ghost!" added Jamie.

Merryn, Matt and Rosie ended up staying with the Fosters for two months. It was a bit of a squash, but Jamie's brother had gone back to university so Merryn had his room while her parents slept in the spare room. They had been overwhelmed by the generosity of the villagers who had donated clothing, bedding – in fact, nearly everything they would need to furnish their new home.

The parish council had been equally as generous, and had offered the family one of the almshouses near to the church. It was a tiny cottage on the end of a terrace with two bedrooms upstairs, a kitchen, lounge and bathroom downstairs. It was shabby and had needed a lot of repairs, hence the long wait in the Fosters' home, but it was fantastic.

As soon as Merryn walked into the house, she felt a warm sense of welcome. Her bedroom at the back of the house overlooked the churchyard. The little postage stamp of a garden spread around to the side of the house, leading to amazing field walks beyond. Plus it was only a fifteen-minute walk along the main road to Jamie's house. Merryn had a feeling that life was starting to look up.

Eight months after the fire, Merryn was sitting on the school field with Jamie, Rob, Marcus, Lily and Maria. They were all watching Ed chat up the new girl in year ten and were laughing at his failure. His reputation had never quite recovered after the Facebook dumping.

"Is everyone still going to the disco tonight?" Maria asked.

Merryn and Jamie looked at each other and shuddered. That evening, there was a celebratory disco at the newly refurbished Assembly Room in Hitcham. Following the fire, Matt had contacted the National Lottery about the grant they had offered him. He explained about the fire at both the hall itself and the houses nearby, and he put a proposition to them. The cost coupled with the new planning regulations had made the possibility of rebuilding the houses pretty much impossible.

The fire had left them penniless. The insurance company were quibbling about paying out because it was a suspicious fire. They claimed that there was evidence of arson, and it was obvious that they suspected Matt had deliberately started the fire to claim on the insurance. Thankfully, the police did not share their suspicions. It looked like a losing battle. So even if a rebuild was possible, there was no cash with which to do it.

Also, there was no way that Matt could get a mortgage on his new salary. He had got a job as an ICT technician at Merryn's high school. The pay was lousy, the perks non-existent, but he loved the job and the holidays even though they were unpaid. Rosie had finished her studying and had secured a part-time job in an accountancy department of a building firm.

Therefore, knowing that no-one would buy the land and feeling that he wanted to help the community who had propped up his family, Matt suggested that the land surrounding The Assembly Room be used for community activities as well.

A joint venture by the parish council and the National Lottery had culminated in the resurrection of The Assembly Room to a place of community use as well as a wild garden area and a football pitch.

It was due to be opened that evening by a local minor celebrity: an actor who, while not particularly famous, made people turn their heads and think, "Where have I seen him before?" Following the opening would be cheese and wine for the adults, then a disco for the youngsters of the village and their friends. Matt had organised the whole event, having asked to be chief custodian of the building.

Although a disco in a village hall was not usually the Mecca of teenage social entertainment, Merryn's friends were all keen to see the new Assembly Room. Merryn and Jamie were not so enthusiastic, however. Usually, Jamie came to visit Merryn as she was still scared of going to her old haunts. But they had to go along.

At six-thirty that evening, Matt took his place as master of ceremonies on the green outside The Assembly Room. It had been rebuilt to look like the former building with its arched windows and slated roof, but it was now clean and straight and exuded an air of pride, not evil. Merryn expected to have her feelings of fear and distrust rekindled when she saw it, but she felt nothing.

The actor, whose name no one could quite remember, made some insipid speech about the value of the community and making the most of the facilities. Everyone clapped politely as he held the scissors over the red ribbon tied on the door. "Just before you make the cut," Matt interrupted, "I would like to add one final thing."

This woke up the on-lookers slightly and they took more interest in this development than the actor's sulky face. "Most of you are aware of the history of this village; the good and the bad. But I feel that we should honour a couple of past residents who made history for reasons beyond their control. Back in 1645, the infamous witch-finder, John Stearne, accused Anne Cricke and Alice Wright of witchcraft. They both died as a result of their questioning even though they were innocent. You may or may not know that I am a descendant of that man, a fact of which I am not proud. I cannot alter the past, but I would like to dedicate this new building to the memory of those two women."

Matt then removed a blu-tacked piece of card from the side of the building to reveal a gleaming brass plaque.

'In memory of Alice Wright and Anne Cricke.

Victims of the witch-hunt of 1645.'

The crowd fell silent for a second, then applause broke out. Few had been aware of the rich heritage of their village; at least now, they had the excuse to find out more.

"How did he know?" Merryn whispered to Jamie. She was so busy looking at her boyfriend for reassurance that she did not notice her father standing behind her.

"I do work at a school, you know," Matt said.

"Yeah, but, how did you know?" Merryn repeated with the fear that had been hidden for months bursting out of her mouth.

"I had to fix the computer in your history teacher's room one day, and he was doing a lesson on witches with some year tens. And I remembered how you used to go on about the witches round here. So I had a chat with Mr Carter and he told me what he knew about the Hitcham witches, and what you had found out. It's really fascinating, you know. But it's like they have been forgotten – there's no acknowledgement of them anywhere. Then I got to thinking; it was my distant relative who had effectively killed those women, so it was up to me to right the wrong. Hence the memorial. Did I do okay?" Matt smiled like a schoolboy who had just got an A star in a test he thought he had failed.

Merryn hugged her father. "You did okay, Dad."

The rest of the proceedings passed successfully. The cheese and wine proved very dull for Merryn and Jamie, so they sneaked across the greensward to his house. "I've got a present for you," he teased as they got in through the front door.

"I remember you saying that nearly a year ago," Merryn giggled.

"May have something to do with you having a birthday every year," Jamie replied.

Merryn suddenly looked sad. "But last year's present is gone. I lost it in the fire."

"I know," said Jamie. He handed her a red jeweller's box, which she slowly opened. Inside was an almost exact replica of the charm bracelet he had bought her the year before, the only difference being that he had added an extra charm – a tiny Labrador. "Sorry, I couldn't wait till next week. I wanted you to have it now, so you could wear it to the disco tonight."

Merryn hugged Jamie with tears in her eyes. Then they rejoined the party that was turning The Assembly Room into a place of celebration – for now.

Other Books by Bryony Allen

Mystery Deceit and a School Inspector, ISBN 0954551095 (2006)

OTOLI, ISBN 9781907728129 (2011)